Shouts split through the air, warning the fire was getting closer.

The frantic crowd and forgotten belongings blocked the roadway ahead. Sophia turned to her mother, who swayed as if she would pass out.

"Mammá!" Sophia dropped the load and ran to her. "We must leave the trunk." Sophia grabbed her mother's arm. Gaining a steady hold, Sophia put a handkerchief in her mother's trembling hand and raised it to her mouth to block the smoke from her lungs.

Mammá surrendered her cherished possession and leaned against her daughter like a wilted flower under the desert sun.

They pushed forward. Sophia didn't know where they were going. Her body ached with every movement. Her empty stomach lurched from the foul air. In that moment of anguish, she allowed silent tears to fall as the world around her turned to ashes.

DIANN HUNT resides in Indiana with her husband. They have two grown children and two grandchildren. Feeling God has called her to the ministry of writing, Diann shares stories of lives changed and strengthened by faith in a loving God.

Trunk
of Surprises

Diann Hunt

Heartsong Presents

To my daughter, Amber Zimmerman, who dreams with me; to my son, Aaron Hunt, who encourages me to do my best; and to my husband, Jim, who is and always will be my hero.

Special thanks to Rosey Dow, Kathleen Paul, and Susette Williams, for their valuable input and endless support. God bless you.

A note from the author:
I love to hear from my readers! You may correspond with me by writing:

Diann Hunt
Author Relations
PO Box 719
Uhrichsville, OH 44683

ISBN 1-58660-621-2

TRUNK OF SURPRISES

All Scripture quotations are taken from the King James Version of the Bible.

Cover illustration by Kay Salem.

PRINTED IN THE U.S.A.

one

Chicago, 1871

The October wind whipped through the dry streets, swirling parched debris through the heavy air. The wisp of a spark appeared. Snatching the tiny ember, the growing winds shoved it aside, spawning giant flames that roared and hissed their way toward the downtown business district.

Sophia Martone coughed as the stench of smoke stretched poisoned fingers into the drafty boardinghouse. She pulled back the sheer curtain and cast a fearful glance at the scene below.

A growing inferno chased frantic people who ran in pandemonium across wooden streets and sidewalks. Desperate citizens clutched their children and valuables, stumbling over one another in their race for safety. Wild horses fled with wagons zigzagging behind. Confusion reigned everywhere the eye could see.

Sophia jerked around to her mother. "Mammá, the fire is coming this way. We must go!"

Regret lined her mother's face as she looked around the room, her gaze lingering on the trunk. She turned and lifted a defiant chin. "We will take the trunk, Sophia."

Sophia nodded. She knew better than to challenge her mother about the twenty-year-old chest. Sophia's father, Luigi, had ordered it custom-made for her mother, Angelica, in Milan, Italy. He had presented it to her with an unexpected gift tucked inside: tickets for America.

Although Sophia couldn't remember the ocean journey, she remembered well the story told to her by her papá many times before. On July 30, 1851, two-year-old Sophia and her parents boarded the *SS Ferruccio* in Genoa with the cherished trunk holding their valuables.

Since that time, the trunk of surprises, as Papá called it, held a place of honor in their home. Before 1860, they never had a Christmas tree, so Mammá brought out the special box every year, decorated it with sprigs of pine and thick red ribbons, and tied a tiny gold bell with string onto the end of the lock.

The little family gave their presents to Mammá, who, with great care, placed the holiday gifts within its walls and locked them for safekeeping until Christmas morning.

When their family began to observe the tradition of having a Christmas tree, Mammá still brought the trunk out and placed it beside the tree.

Sophia could remember her younger days when she would sneak over to the lock on the trunk, trying to figure out a way to open it without the bell sounding. At long last, she would give up, turn, and find her mother standing in the shadows, wearing a playful smile.

Sophia blinked hard to shake the memory. She sighed, her heart heavy with her mother's pain. She walked over to Mammá and placed an arm around her frail, slumped shoulders. Sorrowful eyes looked up to Sophia.

"We will take it, Mammá," Sophia murmured.

Satisfied, Mammá nodded, then wiped her face with a cotton handkerchief as if the entire matter had wearied her. Squaring her shoulders, she hastened to the side of the trunk and curled her fingers around the handle. Sophia hurried to help. Gasping under its weight, the two women hefted the heavy load between them and cautiously edged it down the narrow stairway. The steps creaked and groaned beneath their weight.

They stopped at the bottom of the stairs, where Sophia looked through each room, making sure the boarders were gone. Disheveled rooms told of the occupants' hasty departure.

"I'm sorry, Papá," she muttered under her breath. Sadness

shadowed her thoughts. This had been her home for the last five years. Her father had purchased it for their family, then died eight months later when cholera swept through the city. It killed almost a thousand of its citizens. Sophia had always been thankful he had provided for them even in death. But now. . .

After a quick glance into the last room, Sophia turned as Mammá pulled her hands to her chest. A mournful prayer in her native Italian spilled from her lips.

Sophia yanked on her mother's arm, then called through her own tears, "There is no time for grief, Mammá. We must go!"

With a sorrowful brush of her hand, her mother wiped the tears from her face and stepped toward the only tangible remnant of her past. Quickly, they lifted the trunk. Acrid air, thick with glowing cinders, choked them as they pushed through the entrance and stepped into the chaos of the streets.

"Run to Lincoln Park!" someone yelled over the agonizing noise of the mob.

Sophia looked toward the boardinghouse one last time. Drawing in a ragged breath, she turned back to her mother. They exchanged a painful glance. With reluctance, they left their cherished memories behind and merged with the crowd as they stampeded to safety.

Dense smoke lapped up oxygen along the way. A man staggered past them, overcome by a coughing fit. Sophia and her mother struggled to hold the trunk as frantic people rushed in all directions, bumping and jostling them every which way.

With heavy footsteps, they trudged forward while bluish flames snarled and hissed from fragmented buildings. Deafening screams sliced through Sophia's nerves like a hot knife. Cold chills covered her skin despite the oppressive heat. She watched as exhausted firemen battled in vain to stop the growing inferno at a nearby building.

"Wait, Mammá," Sophia yelled, dropping her side of the trunk. She patted hard against her skirt to smother falling embers as they landed. Bile crawled up her throat, but she refused its torment. She had to be strong for her mother. Sophia clenched her teeth to stop the tears threatening to surface.

"I'm fine, Mammá," she answered before her mother could form the question.

They picked up the trunk once again and plodded farther down the road, occasionally stumbling around burning furniture abandoned in the dusty streets. Sophia's frantic eyes kept constant watch. Like a nervous bird, she scanned the air as the strong winds ripped flaming clothes from abandoned trunks, filling the skies with monstrous torches.

Sophia's head ached from trying to take in the sights around her. People shoveled into hard, crusty ground to bury possessions. Horses ran unbridled through the crowded streets. All around her, scores of people with hollow eyes and tear-streaked faces scrambled to escape.

In an instant, a wagon piled high with carpets, luggage, and paintings raced past them. "Get out of the way!" the driver yelled, cursing the people in his path. As he pushed his way forward, a large chunk of timber fell from a nearby building, startling the man's horses. The frightened animals reared and charged off in another direction.

To her left, Sophia saw a gentleman of apparent wealth load the last of his possessions onto a hired wagon, then count out his cash to the driver. Sophia wished she and her mother had the money to get their trunk to safety. Before she had time to sink further into self-pity, the driver climbed onto his rig, then prompted the horses into action. The rich man shouted, "Not that way, Sir, to the north!" But the driver laughed, waved his dollar bills, and drove out of sight.

Sophia wanted to scream in outrage. Her nerves grew hot at the driver's injustice. She was glad she and her mother didn't have the wealth for a driver, after all. No one would steal their trunk! She bit her lower lip until it hurt. She had to get her mother and the trunk away from here.

Sorrow grew with every step as Sophia and her mother continued ahead. Blistered trees seemed to prophesy of a stark future filled with rubble and ashes. Their scorched fingers mourned the past.

Sophia glanced at the burdensome trunk. It held their few remaining possessions. She tried to shake off her fears. As she turned at a street corner, enormous flames charged toward them. Mammá screamed and dropped the trunk.

Sophia's pulse knocked hard against her temples. "Mammá!" she shrieked through the thick air. Sophia dropped her load and jerked her mother out of the path of danger. Fear pumping her with energy, Sophia maneuvered their trunk to safety around the corner.

They coughed and gasped for air as a screaming woman ran past them, carrying a silent baby in a charred blanket.

Sophia wondered how they could continue. Her thoughts grew as dark as the blackened buildings before them. Mammá interrupted Sophia's despair by grabbing one end of the trunk.

Sophia pulled in a sharp breath as her swollen hands curled around her end of the luggage. Mother and daughter staggered with every step, contending with the weight of the trunk, the rancid smell of scorched remains, and the cruel heat. Mammá stumbled.

"We will rest a moment." Sophia's voice left no room for argument.

Pulling the trunk to a small area off the path, Sophia helped her mother sit on the luggage and catch her breath. Sophia watched her gasp for fresh air, though none could be found. Mammá's graying hair fell in disarray around her weary, crimson face, streaked with smoke and ashes. Her clothes were ripped and sooty. The young woman wanted to spare her mother this sorrow, but she could not.

Sophia wiped her hand across her own stinging eyes. Planning the words she was about to say, she swallowed hard and winced from the pain in her dry throat.

"Mammá, we must leave the trunk."

Her mother turned sharply, lifting flashing eyes to Sophia. "No, my child, we cannot!" Mammá grabbed her daughter's hands. Her wide eyes pleaded for understanding. "It's all we have, Sophia," she said in a cracked whisper, her gaze falling upon the family treasure. "Papá. . ." The words trailed off.

Sophia sighed in desperation and pulled herself up. She glanced at the puffy blisters inside her palms and wondered how she could hang on to the burdensome load any longer. Sophia nodded to her mother, and together they picked up the weight once again.

Shouts split through the air, warning the fire was getting closer. The frantic crowd and forgotten belongings blocked the roadway ahead. Sophia turned to her mother who, at that moment, looked far older than her fifty years. Mammá licked her lower lip and swayed as if she would pass out.

"Mammá!" Sophia dropped the load and ran to her. "We must leave the trunk." Sophia grabbed her mother's arm. Gaining a steady hold, Sophia put a handkerchief in her mother's trembling hand and raised it to her mouth to block the smoke from her lungs.

Mammá surrendered her cherished possession and leaned against her daughter like a wilted flower under the desert sun.

They pushed forward. Sophia didn't know where they were going. Her body ached with every movement. Her empty stomach lurched from the foul air. In that moment of anguish, she allowed silent tears to fall as the world around her turned to ashes.

two

"Wait! I'll help you!" Clayton Hill shouted through the confusion, but the two women didn't hear him. His attention turned to a little boy who rushed to escape the flames spreading up his spine. Just as Clayton started to help, he saw a man nearby dash toward the child. The man threw the boy to the ground and patted him with a blanket until the last spark disappeared. When Clayton shifted back around, the two women were lost in the crowd.

He spotted a neighbor and called out to him. "Mr. York, can you help me pull this trunk onto my wagon? I'm trying to get it to the owners."

"Yes," Mr. York said as he swiped his arm across his forehead. They heaved the trunk onto the wagon while people pushed and scurried around them.

Clayton brushed his hands together a couple of times, then looked up at his neighbor. "May I take you somewhere, Sir?"

"No, no, Clayton. I came to see if the office was still standing, but it's gone." His words held no emotion.

"I'm sorry."

"At least it's insured. That is, if the insurance companies aren't broke by the time this is all over," he said with a grunt. He looked past Clayton. "I've got to go, Boy. My wife is motioning for me. Protect yourself," the older man called over his shoulder, making his way toward his wife.

Clayton climbed onto his wagon. The horses pawed at the ground, frightened by the chaos in the streets. With a tight grip, Clayton struggled with the reins, attempting to hold the animals in check with a sharp tug on the bits.

He began a long search through the mass of smudged faces

for anyone with a vague resemblance to the two women. He wished he had been close enough to see them better.

His search proved futile.

The day soon evaporated as Clayton helped others, delivering families and their belongings to safety.

By evening, the fire had traveled through the north side of the city, incinerating residences and leaving behind a blackened path.

An eerie hush settled upon the streets as the horses trotted closer to Clayton's home. Their *clip-clop* echoed a solemn chant against the night air that reeked of a burning city. Black smoke curled and snaked behind him, taunting him.

Clayton turned his wagon down Park Lane. The scene looked unfamiliar. *This is Park Lane, isn't it?* The street resembled an old picket fence with missing boards.

Clayton felt himself gaping at the pile of rubble that used to be Mariah Wentworth's house.

The reality of the scene unfolded before him as the horses continued at a slow trot. He noticed the Casses' barn had burned to the ground, their house left untouched.

To his right, a few worried neighbors chattered in tiny clusters as they pointed to the darkened sky in the distance. They didn't even seem to notice Clayton. Other neighbors rushed around their property, wetting down houses and prized possessions.

Clayton looked ahead at the road. He hadn't realized the fire came so close to his own street. He slapped the horses' reins in one swift motion and raced toward what he hoped would be his home.

His pulse knocked as hard as the horses' gallop until he came to the large dwelling. Clayton slowed the horses and grabbed his lurching stomach. He took a deep breath to calm himself. "Thank You, God, for sparing our family." The words felt strange upon his tongue. He wasn't used to praying, but it seemed natural to him now.

Coughing hard, Clayton struggled to clear his lungs, but the heavy smoke lingered. He looked once again toward the burning city. With shaking hands, he guided the wagon onto their property.

Clayton unhitched the tired horses, maneuvered them into their stalls, then fed and watered them. Rubbing his hand across the nose of the brown stallion, Clayton's thoughts drifted to the scenes of the day. Images of the thriving city reduced to ashes, helpless people struggling for life, and vagrants preying on the misfortune of others sickened him.

He shook away the memories. With one last pat upon the horse's muzzle, Clayton turned, then noticed the trunk. He considered taking it into the house but decided to wait and see if he and his parents would need to leave soon.

He looked toward the house. His eyelids drooped like heavy blinds over his blurry eyes. The back door appeared miles away. He licked his dry lips and attempted to straighten his slumped shoulders. Staggering from the weight of the day, he took labored steps toward the house. Something wet plopped upon his arm. He looked up, then at his arm again. Within a few seconds, water droplets began to cover him. "It's rain!" he said with disbelief.

Relief sent shocks of energy throughout his exhausted body. He felt as if every nerve, every muscle, awoke with a start from a deep sleep. Hope surged through him, transforming his body like a lifeless flower revived by a light spring rain. He stepped farther into the yard and stopped dead center. Tipping back his head, he exposed his face to the heavens and spread his arms wide, allowing the rain to wash away the weariness of the day. Tears of relief began to mingle with the falling shower.

"Clayton!" The back door slammed behind his mother as she ran to him. "Thank God, you're all right," she cried, wrapping him in a snug embrace.

Clayton's father came running directly behind her, and they

huddled in a circle, crying tears of joy. Gratitude washed over Clayton as his father held the little family close and said a prayer of thanksgiving until the rain forced them inside.

Sitting down at the scrubbed kitchen table, Clayton studied his hands. "I've never seen such a sight, Dad. Twisted metal, ashes, trees stripped of bark, neighborhoods disintegrated with one house left standing." He heard the pain in his own voice.

"And the noise." He shook his head. "People screaming and crying. Popping wood and loud bangs from falling timber. The rich and the poor together in one stew pot, fighting for their lives." Clayton rubbed his neck, feeling his throat tighten with the memory.

"God have mercy on us all," his father responded, shaking his head.

His mother placed coffee in front of Clayton, and he could feel her study him. He glanced at his clothes. His shirt was torn and streaked with smoke and grime. Gray ashes fell from his hair as he rubbed his hand through it. He wiped black soot from his face. Clayton lifted his tired eyes toward her. A weak smile escaped him.

She reached over to pat his hands but stopped midway. "Clayton, your hands are swollen!" she gasped. "You've been burned!" She ran to the cupboard to grab some cream and gauze.

"They're all right, Mom," Clayton drawled with fatigue. But his mother paid no attention. At once, she dabbed the cream on his sore skin and began to wrap his hands with great tenderness.

His father sipped coffee and lowered the cup onto the table. "Although at times it proved inconvenient to be away from the courthouse, I'm glad now that we moved our law practice a distance from town."

Clayton nodded and winced a little as his mother finished wrapping his hands.

His dad added sugar to his coffee and stirred. Staring into

his cup, he continued, "I'm sure business will be down for awhile as people sort through the present disaster." He looked up at Clayton and added, "I may not need you at the office as much." His father stopped stirring, tapped his spoon on the cup's rim, and placed it beside his saucer. Picking up the hot liquid, he sipped as his gaze met Clayton's.

"Good. I was thinking I'd like to volunteer my services to help get the city back on its feet again."

"Wonderful idea."

Clayton couldn't help but notice the look of pride that flashed through his father's eyes. Lost in thought, the two men drank from their cups as Clayton's mother tidied the kitchen.

"Oh, I almost forgot," said Clayton, remembering the trunk in the stable. "I saw two women abandon a trunk on the roadway. I could tell it was valuable to them, but the load was too heavy. They dropped the luggage and ran with the others. I shouted after them, but they didn't hear me. So I loaded the trunk onto my wagon, thinking I could find them, but they disappeared into the crowd. I brought it home. Do you think you could help me bring the case inside, Dad?"

"Sure, Son, but what are you going to do with this mystery box?"

"I don't know. Appears to be of good quality, and I don't want their belongings to get ruined in the stable. I still hope to find those poor women. Maybe something inside will lead me to them—if it opens, of course." Clayton shrugged.

Clayton and his father eased the trunk in from the stable and placed the large box on the kitchen floor. Clayton flinched from the pain in his blistered hand. He was glad his mother didn't notice.

Grabbing a damp cloth, his mother began to clean away a thin film of soot and ashes from the trunk. She turned the bottom up partway and brushed away pieces of hay picked up from the stable.

"A very nice trunk, Son. Beautifully detailed designs." His mother straightened, placed her hands on her hips, and surveyed the final result of her cleaning job. "I would venture to say someone took special care in purchasing this. I hope you do find the owners. I'm sure they're missing it," she said with concern.

"I hope I find them too." He stretched and yawned. "Can we talk more tomorrow? I'm very tired."

"Of course, Dear." His mother's expression softened.

"Do you want to take it to your room until you find the owners?" his father asked.

"Yes. Could you help me again?"

"I'd be glad to." His father reached for the trunk's end. "Clayton, about the trunk. . ." The words had barely rolled off his father's tongue when Clayton's mother put her finger to her mouth and shook her head. His father swallowed the question with a shrug. He threw Clayton the "I guess Mother knows best" look.

Clayton grinned. It wasn't like his mother intimidated his father. Standing five foot, three inches beside his six-foot frame, she was no match for him in size. But they had an understanding: She tended to the domestic matters of the home, while he handled the business affairs.

The plan had worked for their thirty-five years of marriage, and Clayton didn't know of two people who loved each other more.

∗

Clayton felt somewhat refreshed after washing as best he could with bandaged hands. With some effort, he pulled on his nightclothes. He sat on the floor in front of the trunk and ran his fingers across the lid.

The luggage appeared custom-made. The top displayed a large, golden "M." Tiny lines twisted and looped along the edges like a delicate thread.

I wonder if this holds the young woman's trousseau? He

drummed his fingers across his mouth. *No, the older woman seemed the most upset with leaving it. Perhaps the box held her trousseau when she was young? Maybe an heirloom or two rests within its walls.*

After a gentle tug, he was surprised to find the lock unlatched. He lifted the lid, feeling a bit of a snoop for looking inside.

The smell of smoke escaped the opening as he pulled apart items of clothing and miscellaneous possessions. He opened a small wooden box containing a beautiful Nativity set, each piece painted in intricate detail. He sighed and returned the figures inside the box.

Lifting a baby's blanket, he brought the soft pink yarn next to his face. Smoke lingered in the folds. He then pulled out a lacy dress discolored with age. The gown resembled a wedding dress.

His fingers combed through other clothing, then found an old Bible. Picking it up, he gently leafed through the weathered pages. He spotted loose papers filled with verses and comments, a dried flower, and a cryptic note here and there. The family registry page had been documented in pencil. Written names had faded with the passing years. The owner's name listed on the front page said "L" something. The rest of the name, soiled and discolored, would remain a mystery. Clayton closed the Bible and returned the Holy Book along with the other items to their place.

Nothing of real value. Most likely, sentiment drove those women to save this trunk.

Clayton didn't know what he'd expected to find, yet he couldn't help feeling a vague sense of disappointment. As he lowered the lid, something caught his attention. He lifted the top wide again and reached into the right corner, where a slim, delicate book titled "Journal" nestled within the folds of a smooth, yellow blanket.

He looked around the room. *I'm acting foolish. Who cares*

if I look at this? Turning the book over in his hands, he stared at the dark blue binding. His jaw tensed. He opened the cover to see the inner secrets of another. . . .

"My Journal," read the beginning. First entry—

October 12, 1866. Papá died today.

My insides burn with pain. All around me, words swirl with my emotions, taunting me as I reach up to grab them and put them on paper. How can I tell what I feel? How do I express that the most wonderful man in my life is gone forever?

Memories play across my mind, how Papá, Mammá, and I laughed away the hours together.

It doesn't seem real. I expect Papá to walk through my door any moment and kiss me good night. I can almost hear his laughter with Mammá in the other room. Yet as I grab hold of the glorious sound, silence chases it away like a brittle leaf carried on the wind. His laughter is gone. Instead, grief fills the air.

Occupants crowd our boardinghouse, yet the rooms feel hollow and empty, like my heart.

Papá, I cannot bear life without you. What will we do? What is to become of us?

I know I must not cry. Mammá needs me. Her skin is colorless. Her face, vacant. Her eyes, unseeing. Her joy buried with Papá. Sorrow snuffs out our words. Our floors creak and moan. The hall clock ticks, reminding us life goes on. . .but not for Papá. Sometimes I think I can't breathe.

Heavenly Father, will we ever stop hurting? Mammá tries to act brave, but I see the fear in her eyes. Please hold us in Your presence tonight. Only You understand our pain. You never fail us. Thank You.

And Lord, will You hug Papá for me and tell him how much we miss him?

Clayton stared at the page. He reread the last sentence and noticed the ink had blurred the last few words, as if a tear had splattered upon the fragile paper.

His jaw tensed. It would be difficult to lose a parent. He felt an unbreakable bond with his own.

The journal's author revealed a deep faith—something Clayton wished he could claim, but life always demanded too much of him. He had little time for such things.

His thoughts turned back to the two women. Where were they now? At the park?

Clayton's mind paused with the park scene. Desperation and fear lined each face. Children cried. Family members wailed over missing loved ones. Weary, frightened people clamored for food. *Could she have been among them?*

His heart connected with this woman of the journal for reasons he couldn't explain. He decided the two women were mother/daughter. The daughter seemed devoted to family, nurturing. Hadn't she placed protective arms around her mother, pulling her to safety? And her loyalty to her father was evident in her writings.

Clayton knew the little family left behind a great deal when they dropped the trunk. "A lifetime of memories folded into one box," he said, shaking his head. He rewrapped the journal in the blanket and slipped it into place.

Climbing into bed, he glanced once more at the mysterious trunk. The anonymity of it puzzled him. How long he looked at it, he didn't know. At last, Clayton blew out the lantern beside him and settled into an exhausted sleep.

three

Masses of homeless people huddled on the lawn of Lincoln Park. Sobbing, frightened children stumbled through the crowds, searching each face for their families. Sophia wanted to scoop them into her arms and take them all home. But what home? She had nothing to offer them. In an effort to shut out the pain, Sophia closed her eyes and took a deep breath.

Sophia and her mother crumpled onto the ground, leaning against a tree trunk, trying to protect themselves from the chill that seemed to rise with the moon.

Sophia rubbed her mother's arms. "Mammá, are you warm enough?"

Her mother gave a slight nod, then rested her head against the rough bark, her eyes heavy with exhaustion.

Sophia shivered. She willed herself to relax as her mind rambled. Campfires mingled with the stench of the ashen city, burning her nose and parching her throat. She felt her dry, cracked lips with her tongue, longing for a cup of water.

Conversations surrounded her, piercing the night air with raw emotions. Rampant nerves tingled beneath her skin. She had to be strong for her mother. Sophia glanced at Mammá again. Half-dazed with fatigue, she sat, saying nothing.

Just beyond her, a family sought warmth around burning wood. Sophia looked up, watching as the flickering campfire cast an eerie glow across their faces. She glanced around the park. Debris cluttered the area as far as the eye could see.

Such misery. These people have lost everything. Families separated. Agonizing groans circled the night air. Fear seemed to slither in and out of the crowd like a snake. Sophia wanted to run, get away, waken from the nightmare.

"Mammá," Sophia whispered, "look at the buildings." Just then, her mother turned her head in response. In the distance, tall, hollow buildings lifted thick, jagged beams into the moonlit sky.

Mammá shook her head and clicked her tongue. "Luigi would never believe what we have witnessed here today." Sadness filled her voice. "I'm glad he did not see it. He was always full of hopes and dreams. This would hurt him so." She sighed. "Of course, he would offer a reason to give thanks in the midst of it all." She turned to Sophia and gave her a weak smile.

Sophia grinned, remembering Papá's enthusiasm for life and his ever-encouraging words. She longed for him. His joy would have lifted the heaviest of hearts in these dire circumstances.

"Daughter," her mother whispered, breaking through Sophia's thoughts, "did you see the man who loaded the rich lady's trunk on his wagon, the one I pointed out to you?"

"Yes."

"She's standing to our right. I heard her tell someone the man did not meet her. He stole her trunk with all her valuables." Before Sophia could respond, her mother continued, *"Cara Mia,* I wonder where our trunk is tonight."

Sophia grabbed her mother's hand. "I wish I knew, Mammá. I wish I knew."

Mammá shivered. "You are cold." Sophia rubbed her hands with brisk motion across her mother's arms once again.

Suddenly, a gentleman with a kind smile walked over and squatted a few feet in front of them. Dropping some wood, he started a small campfire. "Mother," he called, "do we have a blanket to spare?"

Sophia looked in the direction of the man's gaze. A hefty woman with white hair came toward them with a thick blanket. Her skirt was tattered and worn, her face dirty with soot; but tenderness filled her eyes, revealing a clean heart.

Sophia started to get up, but the woman stretched out her

palm in front of her. "You stay there. I will put this around you." She flipped open the folded blanket, tucking it about Sophia and her mother like a warm cocoon. "We were lucky. We were able to save many things from our home." A thankful smile brightened her face. "We want to share our good fortune with others." Reaching for Mammá's hand, she encouraged, "I hear relief is on the way. They are bringing food and supplies."

"Do they think the fire will stop soon?" Mammá asked in a small, frightened voice.

"No one knows, Dear." The woman stood and gazed toward the burning city. "No one knows." She shook her head, then looked back at Sophia and her mother. "We will be fine. You'll see." Her kindness made Sophia's heart feel lighter.

"Thank you," Sophia called out, but before she could blink, their new friend had already turned to help another.

The warmth of the blanket comforted them. Weary and spent, Sophia and her mother drifted into a restless sleep.

Fire attacked Sophia's dreams, dragging her into a suffocating nightmare. She struggled to breathe. All at once her eyes popped open. A cold drizzle trickled on her face. She blinked, thinking she was still dreaming, when cries began to swell across the park. "It's raining! It's raining!"

The rain showered the crowd with fresh anticipation, bringing people to their feet.

Small circles formed as people huddled, muttering prayers of thanks through their tears. Others started singing. Still others embraced and danced at their campsites. Sleepy children looked on in confusion.

Mourning turned to cheering. Shouts of joy replaced the earlier moans, shattering despair into the night winds.

❧

Sophia had stood in the breakfast line for so long, it was almost lunchtime. Her mother shifted her weight again.

"Mammá, are you feeling all right?"

"I'll be fine, Dear. I'm just a little hungry."

Sophia understood. Her own stomach gurgled and cramped from emptiness. She brushed the thought aside, not wanting to dwell on food.

"Sophia and Angelica!" a woman called as they reached the front of the line.

The two women looked into the kind, wrinkled face of Agnes Baird, a wealthy eighty-two-year-old widow from their church. Strands of snowy white hair fell in loose curls at the sides of her face from a thick bun situated at the top of her head. Sophia thought Mrs. Baird's hair looked like cotton. Her skin resembled soft leather, no doubt from years of working with her flowers. Her kind brown eyes crinkled with her cheery disposition, and her thick middle shook in hearty laughter.

Sophia's heart quickened at seeing the familiar face. "Mrs. Baird, how good to see you!"

Mrs. Baird's expression softened. She turned her head. "Harriet," she called to the woman a few feet away, "could you take over here for a moment, please?" The woman responded at once. She picked up a knife and began to saw thin slices of bread.

Mrs. Baird took Sophia and her mother aside. "How long have you been here?" she asked, her eyes wide, her breath short and quick.

Mammá responded first. "We came here yesterday to escape the fire."

Mrs. Baird shook her head and clicked her tongue. "Oh, my dear, dear friends. I shudder to think you've had to spend a cold night here in this throng of people. No, no, no, it will not do."

Sophia and her mother shared a curious glance.

"You will come home with me." Mammá started to protest, but Mrs. Baird held up her hand. "No use trying to talk me out of it, Angelica, 'cause my mind's made up." Before

Sophia or her mother could utter another word, Mrs. Baird grabbed some food for her friends and said to her coworker, "Since you have enough helpers today, Harriet, I'll be back tomorrow. I've some urgent matters to tend to right now."

Harriet offered a quick wave, then busied herself once more with her tasks.

Within minutes, Mrs. Baird had whisked Sophia and her mother into a carriage, and they were well on their way to Mrs. Baird's home on Park Lane.

❧

"If you'll follow me, I'll take you to your rooms," Mrs. Baird said once they had finished their tour of the lower level.

Sophia tried not to gawk as she and her mother followed the older woman across plush rugs that hugged the hardwood floors and climbed a winding, oak staircase toward the bedrooms. Their friend's home was more beautiful than Sophia had imagined. Though not a mansion, the massive Victorian home stretched into many rooms decorated with beautiful furniture and tasteful paintings.

Sophia stared in disbelief when she stepped inside the room designated for her. Her gaze took in the rich colors, the thick covers draped across the large feather bed and plump down pillows lining the headboard. The moment she looked upon the corner fireplace, she stiffened. Scenes from the city's fire flashed ghostlike upon the hearth's flames. A thick log shifted, dropping farther into the blaze, causing the painful visions to flee. The smell of pine scented the room, calming her. She allowed her mind to wander to days of her childhood when her father read their family Bible beside the warmth of their fireplace. She would not allow the recent tragedies to rob her of those joys nor mar her future. She shook off her musings and took in the rest of the room. Looking up, Sophia felt heat climb her cheeks when she saw Mrs. Baird watching her.

"Do you like it, my dear?" The older woman's eyes twinkled.

"Oh, Mrs. Baird, it's—why, it's beautiful." Sophia turned and hugged her friend, catching a whiff of lemon verbena.

"Mi scusi."

Mrs. Baird looked up as Mammá entered the room. "Does she always talk like that?"

Sophia donned a playful expression and nodded.

"I suppose I'll have to learn some Italian now."

"I'm afraid so." Mammá joined in. "And 'spaghetti' does not count."

Sophia blurted out a giggle, then covered her mouth at once. The older women joined in as the trio descended the stairway.

⁂

After dinner, Mrs. Baird picked up her cup of tea from the table. "Won't you join me in the sitting room?"

Sophia and her mother poured a cup and followed their friend.

"I've decided one can get by without many things in this life, but evening tea is an absolute must," Mrs. Baird said as she settled into her favorite polished oak rocker. Sophia and her mother eased onto the dark velvet settee across from Mrs. Baird. The furniture snuggled together in a semicircle around the warmth of the hearth.

Mrs. Baird stirred her drink. Tucking a bent finger into the handle, she lifted the hot liquid to her lips and took a quick sip. A comfortable pause lingered.

"I heard there's been looting in the city," said Mrs. Baird, placing her cup in the saucer with a delicate clink. "Such goings-on, I've never seen." She shook her head in disgust.

"People do desperate things when they are hungry," Mammá said with her usual compassion.

Mrs. Baird's expression revealed less mercy. "True, but some of those scoundrels are just people preying on the misfortune of others."

"It is a sad thing." Mammá's words were void of judgment.

"I have it from a good source that troops are volunteering to come and help us. Of course, that's not confirmed, mind you." Mrs. Baird took another swallow of tea.

"Many people speak of leaving the city," Sophia added.

"Right. I have a friend in the railroad business, Thomas Medill, and he tells me the railroads are offering free rides out of town." Mrs. Baird rocked slowly in her chair. "He says they have to be sick, aged, or have a large family to qualify. And women and children are allowed to go." She stopped rocking. "Now don't you two go getting any ideas."

Mammá laughed, causing Mrs. Baird's frown to change into a smile.

Sophia marveled that their dear friend knew so many influential people. No doubt it was the result of all her volunteer work. Without question, the older woman was an asset to the community.

The mantel clock chimed eight, breaking the silence. Burning logs crackled in the fireplace, catching Sophia's attention. She watched the dancing flames.

"Time will tell the devastation our city has been through," Mammá offered thoughtfully, her voice filled with concern. She looked to Mrs. Baird. "And we thank God for sending you to us in our time of need. Otherwise, we would be among those who are homeless."

"For pity's sake!" Mrs. Baird waved her hand. "I'm glad to help. Been going to the same church for many years now. You're like my family. I could never leave you out in the cold. Luigi would have my hide when I entered the pearly gates," she added with a chuckle.

Mamma smiled with gratitude.

The evening continued in pleasant conversation and before Sophia knew it, the mantel clock announced the bedtime hour.

four

Only a few days after the fire, the city bustled with a mingling of volunteers and needy people trying to bring calm and order to their town once again. Clayton tied his horse at the hitching post and walked toward the First Congregational Church on Washington and Ann Streets. Scores of townsfolk stood in line, waiting for food, water, and clothing. The trail began at the top of the church steps and traveled down the road for almost a block.

People coming out of the building carried stacks of clothing, bedding, and food supplies.

"Hey, Aaron," one man yelled out to someone leaving the church, "do they have enough for all of us?" The crowd within earshot listened for his response.

A wide grin stretched across Aaron's face. He shifted his load and responded, "They sure do. I hear supplies are coming in from everywhere, even New York!"

Some cheered.

A man behind Aaron called out, "They're offering free train tickets for people who can't work for themselves and want to leave town. Ask in there—they'll tell you."

A soft murmuring rippled through the crowd. Clayton excused his way through the throng of people.

"Hey, no cutting in, Mister," someone said, reaching out to shove him away.

"I'm a volunteer," Clayton responded with haste, knowing these people were tired, restless, and hungry. It wouldn't take much to upset them.

A few of them eyed him with suspicion, then shrugged and let him through to the front entrance.

Pungent body odors assaulted Clayton's senses the moment he entered the church. He turned when he heard a child cry out. A volunteer doctor pulled the needle from the child's arm and applied a bandage. The doctor tousled the little one's hair, then looked up and shouted, "Next." A sign on the table said, "Get smallpox vaccines here."

Clayton continued walking through the maze of confusion, hearing instructions and calls for help flying around him.

"Sir, here's an application for employment. We need help all around the city, so there are jobs available," the woman behind the table said to the middle-aged man.

The man tapped his finger to his forehead and thanked her.

A blond volunteer reprimanded the heavyset woman in front of her, "Ma'am, when that runs out, you may come back for more. We will not give you any more today. We want to make sure there's enough for everybody."

Clayton traveled into a side room where people searched through piles of clothes and shoes.

"Ma'am, how tall did you say your daughter was?" the worker asked as she rummaged through some clothes. Clayton exited the room before he heard the response.

In the next room, relief workers filled mattresses with hay and cornhusks and passed out the bedding to the homeless. Clayton overheard two women discussing that mattresses were coming in from local upholsterers for distribution at the rate of three hundred to four hundred daily.

"May I help you, Sir?"

Clayton turned to face an aged woman who was so thin, he felt sure if he exhaled too deeply, he would blow her over. Her faded blue eyes smiled up to greet him. He cleared his throat. "Yes, Ma'am. I was wondering if I could be of some help around here."

No sooner were the words spoken than the little woman clamped her hands together, and her mouth spread into a wide snaggletoothed grin. "Oh, yes," she assured him. "We can use all the help we can get!" She tugged at his jacket, pulling him to a workstation.

Clayton wondered what he had gotten himself into.

❧

Slipping quietly into his room at day's end, Clayton closed the door behind him and prepared for bed. He could hardly wait to rest his aching muscles. Though tired and spent, he felt compelled to lift the lid of the trunk. Once settled, he pulled out the journal and turned the pages to where he had left off the night before.

November 1st. Almost three weeks since Papá died. I think the laughter died with him. Mammá walks around the house with a sad face. Every night is the same. She cooks meals for the boarders, then goes to her room.

She tries to encourage me, but her smile does not reach her eyes. I no longer go to school, and I try to help with the chores as much as I can.

I've been sewing for one of the ladies at church. As soon as she discovered I could make dresses, she started bringing fabric over to our house, requesting me to make clothes for her. I enjoy making clothes, and the money helps Mammá and me to get along.

One day I think I will try to make dresses like the ones from Paris, France! I will open a store and sell them!

Mammá would scorn me for talking such nonsense, but Papá would chuckle and give me a hug, telling me it is a good thing to dream big. He would say, "God put the dream in your heart, Bambina, and He expects you to do your part with it."

Papá said he and Mammá came to America carried by dreams.

I miss you, Papá. How I wish you were here. No one dreams with me the way you did.

Clayton closed the book. Sadness tugged at his heart in a way he couldn't explain. It was as if he could feel this young woman's pain.

"I must be crazy to get involved like this with a faceless person," he said out loud. He blew out the lantern and climbed into bed, muttering, "And I'm crazier for talking to myself."

❧

Sophia found herself at the church relief center with Mrs. Baird.

"Come this way, Sophia," Mrs. Baird yelled behind her. Sophia pushed through the crowds of people, trying to keep up with the energetic woman. They came to an abrupt halt in front of a frail, petite woman with eyes full of spunk.

"Martha Adams, this is Sophia Martone, and she would like to help," Mrs. Baird said in a matter-of-fact manner. "Do you have a place for her?"

Sophia chuckled to herself at Mrs. Baird's no-nonsense approach.

The little woman nodded with enthusiasm. "We could use help in the sewing room. We've received almost five thousand sewing machines, and we need to match them with worthy recipients."

Before Mrs. Baird could respond, the woman whisked Sophia away toward her workstation. Mrs. Baird headed in the direction of the door. Waving her hankie, she called over her shoulder, "I'll pick you up this afternoon, Dear." Sophia returned the wave and wondered where these two women got their energy.

Sophia's eyes widened with the scenes around her. The flurry of activity made her feel dizzy. She followed the old woman into a room cluttered with new sewing machines and a stack of applications. Sophia knew a little about the machines. Some time ago, one of the wealthy ladies for whom Sophia had sewn needed two dresses in a short time. The woman had kindly offered the use of her own machine to Sophia to aid in the quick completion of her dresses. Sophia still marveled at the incredible machine. Never could Sophia have imagined so many owning their own machines. The generosity of others pouring into the needy city amazed her.

Sophia took a deep breath. Before she had time to consider the volume of work, Mrs. Adams grabbed her arm.

"I have someone you need to meet," she said as she practically pulled Sophia across the room. "This person oversees everything. If there's anything you need in the way of supplies or time to catch your breath, anything at all, this young man will be happy to assist you. Let him know."

Sophia looked around as they made their way to the other side. When they stopped, she turned her face from the older woman and lifted her gaze into the darkest eyes she had ever seen. Did she catch a flicker of amusement in them?

"Sophia Martone, this is Clayton Hill."

The young man held himself in a dignified manner, as one with education and proper upbringing, yet a boyish quality emanated from him. He didn't appear standoffish like the intellectual and rich sometimes did, but rather had an approachable way about him—a kind, friendly manner.

Sophia realized her mouth was gaping and promptly snapped it shut.

"Nice to meet you, Ma'am," Clayton said, a broad smile stretching across his face.

❧

The cool air held the slightest hint of dampness and still smelled of a burned city. Gray clouds loomed in thick piles across the morning sky when Mrs. Baird's driver, Ben Higgins, pulled the carriage around to the front of the house.

Sophia stopped before climbing aboard and looked toward him. "Thank you, Mr. Higgins, for doing this for me."

"Glad to be of help, Miss."

She nodded and lifted her skirts to step into the carriage.

Mr. Higgins clicked his tongue, prompting the horses into action, and they made their way through the streets toward the area where Sophia and her mother had left the trunk. Not knowing what to expect, Sophia chewed on her lip in anticipation. She wondered if the trunk would be there. If she did find it, would it be fire damaged or, worse yet, reduced to ashes?

Sophia lifted her chin and straightened her back. She would not allow her thoughts to travel that road. Papá would never approve. No matter what the outcome, she would manage somehow.

The carriage meandered through the unfamiliar sights of splintered remnants of yesterday's prosperity. Sophia sighed. Heaviness swelled within her. Dark shadows hovered through the quiet downtown that once had been alive with trading and gala events. Temporary shanties now emerged through the gray ashes where proud buildings once stood.

She felt thankful the Relief Society had provided the necessary wood for people to build these temporary homes until more permanent dwellings could be erected. Hammers pounded even now as men worked to construct the tiny structures for their families.

The carriage halted, and Sophia climbed down. "Is this the place, Miss?" the driver asked.

"Yes, Mr. Higgins, I think so." Sophia scanned what used to be familiar territory. She couldn't help but wonder if this was the right area. Familiar landmarks had disintegrated. One site looked like another, masses of charcoal and smoldering debris everywhere the eye could see.

"Would you like to survey the area, Miss? Perhaps you left it farther down the road?"

She looked again at Mr. Higgins. "Thank you." Sophia appreciated his patience and kindness. Though fairly new to his job with Mrs. Baird, the driver had come to her with fine recommendations. "A real blessing," that's what Mrs. Baird called him. Sophia couldn't agree more.

She looked again at Mr. Higgins. "Thank you." She eased back into the carriage, and they continued their search.

five

Workers busied themselves at the Relief Center, helping people as they arrived. Quiet conversations rippled throughout the workstations as Sophia sat at her table, staring ahead at nothing in particular, thinking of her drive through the city streets the day before.

Disappointment washed over her anew with the realization that their family trunk was gone. . .forever.

"Miss?" A woman interrupted her thoughts.

Sophia snapped to attention. "Oh, I'm sorry. Here's the form," she said, extending an application for a sewing machine to a young woman with ragged clothes and large, grateful eyes. The woman thanked her and turned to find a place to write.

Clayton walked from behind Sophia and pulled a chair up to the table. "You holding up all right?"

Sophia wiped her forehead with a handkerchief, then turned to face at him. "Yes, thank you. I'm fine." Their eyes locked for an instant. Sophia could feel her face growing warm and instantly looked away.

"Seems it never slows down around here," Clayton offered.

"I know. I think we're getting the help to the citizens, though. People don't seem quite as desperate as before."

Clayton leaned back, tipping his chair. He seemed to study her. "I saw someone who looked like you on Park Lane yesterday. Was it you?" His eyes sparked with interest.

Sophia thought for a moment. Having learned from Mrs. Adams that Clayton was an attorney of substantial means, Sophia didn't want to fill him in on her background. What would he think if he knew of her poverty, her homeless plight if not for Mrs. Baird? "Well, yes, I–I live there." She bit the corner of her lip as guilt tugged at her. After all, she did live there. She needn't explain.

"Really?" His eyes grew wide. His chair dropped to the floor. "I do too!" he added with enthusiasm.

Sophia's heart sank. Now she'd gotten herself into a fix.

"It seems odd I've never noticed you before. I mean, I'm sure I would have noticed—I mean—" He broke into a crooked smile as he stumbled for the words.

"I understand," Sophia interjected.

Martha Adams approached them, bringing chitchat of the day. Sophia allowed her thoughts to wander, thankful that Mrs. Adams had interrupted their conversation.

Sophia looked at Clayton as he conversed with the little woman. His thick, dark hair lay across a broad forehead. He had a strong jaw, compelling, dark eyes, and firm features. There was a rugged handsomeness about him.

"Don't you agree, Miss Martone?" Mrs. Adams asked.

Sophia blinked. "Oh, yes, Ma'am." She wondered what she had agreed to. When would she learn that daydreaming always got her into trouble?

An applicant drew her away from the conversation, and before she could slip into any more musings, her workday had ended.

ꙮ

Clayton attempted to read a book, but Sophia's face kept popping up on the page. He thought of the way she swept her black hair back and pinned it at the nape of her neck, allowing a few loose tendrils to escape dainty hairpins and fall across her forehead. Her deep brown eyes had mesmerized him from the start. The complexion of her oval face, though a bit pale, looked as soft and delicate as a fragile wildflower.

His mother looked up from her quilting. "You haven't turned the page in over an hour."

"Hmm?" Clayton lifted a vacant gaze to her.

"The page of your book—you haven't turned it in quite some time."

"Oh," Clayton said. "I was thinking."

His parents exchanged a wink.

He looked at them, puzzled. "Am I missing something?"

Mother poked her needle back into the quilted cover, pulling the thread through in even stitches. "Oh, nothing," she teased. "We were thinking about the nice young lady we saw you talking with at the Relief Center. Maybe you were thinking of her too?" She stopped sewing and looked at him. Her eyebrows raised, and her eyes held a hint of mischief.

He looked at his grinning father. "Yeah, she's nice," admitted Clayton, all at once feeling like a schoolboy with his first crush.

"What's her name?" His father laid aside his newspaper and looked at him with interest.

Clayton decided he wasn't going to get any reading done. He slipped a marker in his book and closed it. "Sophia Martone. She lives somewhere on this street, but I'm not sure where. I can't imagine why I haven't noticed her before." He shook his head to clear his thoughts. "Anyway, we've gotten to know each other over the past few weeks, working together. She's quite pleasant."

His mother picked up her sewing once again. "Why don't you invite her for dinner?"

Clayton looked surprised. "Do you think I should?"

"Why not?" Delight flickered in her eyes. "We'd like to meet her."

Clayton and his mother decided on a date, and he made a mental note to ask Sophia the next day.

❧

The following morning, Sophia wondered at Martha Adams's expression when she called all of the workers together for a meeting. Those around Sophia chatted about various topics, but she watched Mrs. Adams. The woman seemed different today, like she had aged a few years overnight. Her shoulders slumped, and her mouth formed a tense line.

"Ladies and gentlemen, please be seated," Mrs. Adams said, taking her place in front of them. "It's unfortunate that I need to call this meeting. You have worked with diligence, and the leaders of our town have expressed their appreciation for all you have done to put Chicago back on its feet." She paused and looked away as if gathering the nerve to speak further. Taking a deep breath, she looked at them once again. "There's a matter we need to address." She squared her shoulders and lifted her chin. "There's no cause for alarm, but we need to take the necessary precautions," she stated with a calm voice as she scanned the crowd.

"The fact of the matter is, a man who comes to our facility has come down with cholera."

A gasp rippled through the crowd. Sophia felt as though she had been punched in the stomach. She couldn't face another epidemic like the one that had taken Papá.

Mrs. Adams held up her hand to silence the restless workers. "No need to be afraid. The doctor wanted me to announce it so we might take extra precautions. Since the city upgraded the water system after the last outbreak, we should be fine. Our concern is with the homeless who have been living in dire circumstances."

In the back, a young woman with a head full of red curls raised her hand.

"Yes, Sarah?"

"How do we prepare? What must we do?"

All eyes in the room stared at Mrs. Adams like she was a judge about to pronounce sentencing. "We must wash our hands without fail on a regular basis. Never put your fingers next to your mouth. Try not to touch anyone's clothing. When we find out a person is infected, we will take measures to burn their bedclothes and sterilize their surroundings. The doctors are also on call with available medicines." She glanced at the shelf clock and sighed. "I'm afraid that's all the time we have for now. If you have further questions, see me after we close tonight. Thank you."

A solemn mood swept over the group as they shuffled to their workstations. Sophia tried to busy herself with applications so she wouldn't think about the disease. Still, she wondered if she should handle the papers. She would wash her hands right after she finished with the forms.

Upon hearing Clayton's voice across the room, she looked up. She watched him as he offered encouragement to a man in need. His kindness surprised her. She would expect a wealthy young attorney like him to be snobby and uncaring, but he wasn't like that. He volunteered endless hours and energy, always putting other people first.

She liked him a lot. An involuntary smile formed on her lips.

The man turned and walked out of the room. Sophia started to wave at Clayton, but as he turned around, he placed a hand against his stomach, grimaced, and bent over. Sophia gasped. Clayton straightened himself and looked around, as if making sure no one saw him. Not wanting to embarrass him, Sophia lowered her head so he wouldn't find her looking.

When she glanced up again, he was walking toward her. "Hello," he said when he reached her table.

Her eyes met his. "Hello." His skin looked pasty. Dark circles emphasized the dull color of his eyes. *Why am I worrying about him? I've got to stop this. He's overworked, that's all.*

He pulled up a chair. "Are you somewhere else?" Clayton teased, his smile never reaching his tired eyes.

"Oh, I'm sorry," Sophia replied. "I think I'm a bit weary." She couldn't pull her gaze away from him. He looked sick.

A concerned silence stretched between them. Sophia wondered if he was thinking about the cholera announcement. As if he read her thoughts, he spoke up.

"Sure hope the cholera doesn't get as bad as it did a few

years back. Do you remember that outbreak? People were frantic. No one knew where it would strike next."

She remembered, but she didn't feel like talking about it. Sophia nodded. She felt his gaze fix upon her.

"Are you all right, Sophia?" He lifted her name like a soft breeze.

Her heart filled with warmth. "I'm fine." She felt thankful for his concern. "How are you keeping up with everything?"

"I'm somewhat exhausted, I must confess, but I think I'll make it." A weak smile crossed his lips.

She returned his smile, wishing with all her might that she could believe it was mere fatigue that plagued him. His nearness sent her heart fluttering. She mustn't worry. *Everyone's overcome by the sheer volume of work. That's all it is.* She passed out another application to a woman who stopped at the table.

Clayton fidgeted in his seat. Sophia tried not to notice, yet she wondered if there was something on his mind.

"Sophia, I was thinking about—well, actually, I was hoping that maybe—what I mean to say is—" He coughed. At last, he regained his composure. "I'm not doing this very well, am I?"

She attempted to encourage him with a smile. What was he trying to say? Anticipation fixed her in place, daring her to breathe.

Clayton swallowed hard. He looked straight into her eyes. "Sophia, would you consider coming to my home for dinner—" Before he could finish his sentence, he clutched his stomach and tumbled from the chair.

Fear seized Sophia. Her scream ripped through the air as Clayton's body landed hard against the cold wooden floor.

Someone shouted, "Cholera!" Pandemonium broke loose. People scattered in all directions, yelling, shoving, and knocking over supplies. The frantic crowd burst through the front doors and exited the building.

Panic washed over Sophia. But not because of the cholera scare. She feared for Clayton. Would he die like Papá? Could his life come to an end so soon? Nausea filled her. She had to stop thinking like this. Reaching deep within, she drew a long breath, trying desperately to find strength in it. With weak knees, Sophia knelt beside Clayton's still body. Lifting trembling fingers, she stroked the moist, dark hair from his bloodless face, barely aware when the doctors rushed through the doors.

six

Though most nights Sophia looked forward to drinking tea in the sitting room with her mother and Mrs. Baird, tonight Sophia's heart longed for solitude. Even the burning logs in the fireplace failed to warm her. Thoughts of Clayton swirled through her anxious mind. She could think of nothing else.

Mammá stirred her tea. "You are worried about your friend, Sophia?"

"Yes," Sophia answered in a small voice.

"I talked to Mrs. Adams," Mrs. Baird offered. "They are hopeful he is improving."

Sophia said nothing. She knew what the disease had done to her papá. All the dormant fears surrounding Papá's death resurrected like phantoms to wreck havoc upon her spirit.

Mammá, seeming to read her thoughts, reached over and touched Sophia's hand. "It's different this time, *Cara Mia*. They know more about the disease. Besides, they're not even sure he has cholera."

"Yes, Mammá." Sophia fidgeted in her chair and tried not to think about it.

Mrs. Baird attempted to brighten the mood. "Did you hear the story about the cow starting the fire?"

Mammá took a swallow of tea and nodded. "Poor soul. If the story is true, the owners carry around much sorrow. If it's not true, they're shamed just the same."

"And think of the poor cow—he's bound to become somebody's dinner!" Mrs. Baird said with a laugh, triggering a hearty shake around her ample midsection.

Sophia looked at her mother, who was trying to stifle a chuckle, until the three chortled right out loud.

Dear Mrs. Baird. She's trying to keep my thoughts from Clayton. I wonder how he's doing. . . .

❧

Clayton's own groaning woke him. Where was he, anyway? His clouded mind moved in and out of dreams filled with scrubbed rooms and white-coated workers.

"Mom," he heard himself say in a weak, unfamiliar whisper.

Clayton tried to lift his head and look around, but the blurry room started to spin. His stomach lurched. He heard his mother's voice call through what seemed a long tunnel, "I'll get the nurse."

Nurse? Where's Dad? Where am I? Don't leave, Mom. What's going on?

The silent questions remained unanswered. His heavy eyelids surrendered to an unknown demand, and he drifted once again into the dark place where time stood still.

❧

Light beams pushed through the thinning branches of a thick oak tree outside the window and sprayed into Clayton's bedroom, causing him to stir. His eyes popped open from the brightness. He tried to focus.

"Good morning, Sleepyhead." His mother got up from the rocker she must have brought into his room. She laid her Bible on the stand and walked over to him.

"Mom." He started to speak, but his throat felt raw. He couldn't lift himself. His questioning eyes met hers.

"You've been very sick, Clayton. We almost lost you." His mother patted his shoulder.

He stared at her, trying to make sense of her words.

"The doctor told us he felt you were through the worst of it, and we brought you home from the hospital yesterday, though I wonder at his wisdom." Concern colored her eyes.

Clayton tried to talk again. He lifted his head a little, thought better of it, and eased back down on his bed.

"Shh, don't try to talk, Dear." She gave his arm a gentle

squeeze. "You'll be fine, but you're going to need plenty of rest. Your body is weak from lack of food, but you'll be up in no time." She bent down and kissed his forehead. "Would you like a drink of water or anything?"

Clayton shook his head. Right now, all he wanted to do was sleep.

"I'll let you rest for awhile. When you wake up, I'll bring you some broth." She tiptoed from his room and, without making a sound, closed the door behind her.

ها

Although thankful Clayton survived his illness, Sophia filled her days with work so she couldn't think about him. The fear of losing him exposed her true feelings. She struggled to hide them, shove them away, deny them. Where would they take her? Would they cause her more pain? Did he care about her? Could she fit into his world? He was inviting her to dinner when he got sick. Would he ask her again? Uncertainties shadowed every thought.

Mrs. Adams interrupted Sophia's inner turmoil. "Sophia, Emily will fill in for you. I want you to follow me."

Sophia looked at Emily, then back at Mrs. Adams. She rose from her chair and walked behind Mrs. Adams. They found an empty room and sat in facing chairs.

Mrs. Adams placed her knobby fingers over Sophia's hand. "You look tired, my dear. I want you to get some rest."

Sophia tried to brighten her expression, but she couldn't muster the energy. "I'm fine, really." She attempted to sound convincing.

Mrs. Adams shook her head. "You've been working hard. Your days are too burdensome for one so young." Mrs. Adams's kind eyes warmed Sophia. "The doctors assure me the cholera scare is over. I'm not sure if they ever decided Mr. Hill had cholera, but I am told he is recovering nicely."

A heart swelled with gratitude choked out Sophia's response.

"Thank God, we didn't have a cholera outbreak like the one

in '66. This time it was very controlled. Only a few deaths, from what I understand. God rest their souls." Mrs. Adams blotted her forehead with an embroidered handkerchief.

Sophia kept silent, still not wanting to discuss the dreadful time in her life when the disease had taken her papá.

Mrs. Adams stared at her with concern. "We have plenty of workers. I'd like you to go home."

Sophia started to protest, but her aching muscles talked her out of it. "Yes, Ma'am," she agreed with reluctance.

Mrs. Adams patted her hand. "I'll see you on Monday." With that, she stood and ushered Sophia through the door.

❧

Clayton propped himself up in his bed. He sipped some broth. He could feel his strength returning. After he finished lunch, he placed the tray with the bowl and silverware on his stand.

Easing himself from his mattress, Clayton crawled over to the trunk. Although somewhat stronger, his weakened body still trembled.

After opening the lid, he pulled out the familiar journal, then closed the trunk. With the book tucked at his side, he made his way back to bed just as someone knocked on the door.

He slipped the journal under his covers. "Come in."

"Good. You've finished the broth," his mother said, lifting the tray from his stand. "You're feeling better, then?" Her eyes bore into him for the truth.

"Much better. Thank you."

Her shoulders relaxed. "Good."

Clayton studied his mother. Against her pale skin, the half circles beneath her tired eyes gave her a ghostly appearance. She turned to leave the room.

"Mom, thanks for all your help. I know it's been rough on you the past few weeks."

She turned to him.

"That's why God made mothers, Dear." She winked.

"Anyway, I'm thankful God has spared you, and the worst is behind us." Her tenderness comforted him. "You get some rest." She closed the door behind her.

Clayton considered her words. God had spared him, and he didn't know why. Clayton thought his own strength and wisdom had carried him through life up to this point, and he never felt the need to call upon God. Yet in recent days, he found himself thinking of Him more and more.

It wasn't that he didn't believe; he just didn't care one way or the other. He went to church with his parents, but the extent of his faith stopped there. That's why the journal intrigued him. The personal relationship this writer seemed to have with God moved him in a way he had never before experienced.

Memories of his parents reading their Bibles came to him. He remembered the time he happened upon them as they prayed at the kitchen table. He just never took it seriously.

His thoughts traveled to the journal.

Reaching in, he pulled the book out from underneath his covers. Casting a quick glance at the door, he made sure it was closed. Satisfied with his privacy, he opened the journal and flipped to the next entry.

December 5. It's been so long since I've been able to write. Mammá and I work night and day for the boarders. Something happened the other night with one of the tenants.

The boarders were gone—all but one young man, who stayed in his room. Mammá had stepped into the kitchen, leaving me in the sitting room. This big man walked in and approached me from behind.

"I have been watching you," he said in a strange voice. Oh, my stomach churns with the thought of it! Then he did the most despicable thing. He turned me around to face him and tried to kiss me!

Mammá walked in as I was struggling to free myself

from his grasp. Mammá raged in Italian and chased him around the furniture with a broom. The broom was as big as Mammá, but she thrashed at him as hard as she could, missing every time, but coming close enough to make him jump and let out a "Whoop!"

When I think of that big man running away from such a little woman, I have to laugh.

Clayton grinned as he pictured the scene in his mind.

The boarder grabbed things from his room as fast as he could, never to return again. Mammá hugged me for a long time while I cried.

"If only Papá were here," I told her.

Mammá said our heavenly Papá was with us, and He would help us like my papá would have done. I felt better then, and we prayed together.

Oh, I almost forgot! Mammá pulled the trunk out today! She thinks I didn't see, but I heard her scooting it and peeked around the corner. She pulled it into her bedroom, as she does every year, to prepare for Christmas.

Gifts for only two people will fill it this year. The big trunk will have much room to spare. Though, I suppose Mammá will make gifts for the boarders as always.

Clayton thought on her words. What was she like? Vulnerable. Caring. Deeply passionate for those whom she loved. This young girl was at least old enough for a gentleman to notice. Must be pretty, or the man wouldn't have been interested. His heart quickened. *I'm being foolish. I'll never find her.* Feeling too tired to get up, he stuffed the book under his pillow.

Frustration creased his brow. His teeth ground hard with his thoughts. He had to find her, but how?

❧

"Are you sure you're up to being here?" Mrs. Adams asked with a worried frown.

"I'm much better, but I have a specific reason for coming," Clayton said.

Mrs. Adams offered her full attention.

He wondered if Mrs. Adams would give him the information. "I was hoping to see the card list of the names of people who have been staying in Lincoln Park."

"Oh. We do have a list of everyone who has come in here, from the first day we opened," Mrs. Adams stated, looking proud of her organizational skills.

She still hadn't answered his question. Clayton tried to look impressed, which seemed to encourage her.

"I don't know if you've noticed, but the people write their names on a card and carry it with them to each room where they receive supplies. The worker writes what they've received on the card and the date, and the people then have to drop the card off to the last table before leaving."

Clayton smiled to himself. He knew the process well. He just didn't know if and where the shelter kept the cards. But he kept silent, not wanting to deny her the joy of sharing her expertise.

"Sarah has the cards in a box on the far right table. Tell her you need to go through them."

His heart quickened. "You are wonderful, Mrs. Adams!" Clayton said, grabbing her shoulders and bending down to give her a peck on her forehead. She wobbled for a moment; but before she could comment, he was at Sarah's table.

❧

Clayton pored over card after card, but he could find nothing matching his mother/daughter team. Maybe they went to the Sands, another place of refuge in the city for the homeless. No, no, that would be too far away from where he saw them. They had to be at Lincoln Park. He drummed his fingers on the table. *Of course,* he reasoned, *maybe they found other family members and are staying with them.* His fingers came to an abrupt halt. *If that's true, I'll never find her.* A weary sigh escaped him. He rubbed his aching neck muscles. *I feel like I'm chasing dreams.*

"Clayton, hello!" Sophia came up to his table. Her dark eyes sparkled. She looked as refreshing as a bright red apple on a crisp, autumn day.

His heart turned over with the sight of her. "Hello," he returned, standing to greet her.

"May I sit down with you?" She fanned herself.

"Please." Clayton pulled out the seat across from him. Except for a couple of people tending to duties at the opposite end, the room provided a quiet setting in which they could talk.

"Thank you." She pulled off her bonnet and laid it on her lap. "So, what are you doing here?"

Clayton took his seat across from her. "Just. . .dreaming," he answered in truth.

"Oh? Someone once told me it's good to dream." Amusement flickered in her eyes as her fingers moved loose dark curls back in place.

Clayton studied her for a moment.

"How have you been, Clayton?" she asked in a whisper, running her fingers along the edge of her bonnet.

"I'm fine. . .now," he said, his gaze fixed on her.

She looked down at her bonnet and twirled the ties. "I'm glad you're better. I—"

"You are?" His brows arched as he tilted his head to look into her eyes.

A soft crimson climbed her cheeks, making her lovelier than ever.

She brushed her hand across her lap, causing her bonnet to fall on the floor. They both reached down to pick it up. She grabbed the bonnet as his palm cupped over hers. Their eyes locked once again, neither saying a word.

Sophia looked down and politely slipped her fingers from his grasp.

"Thank you for caring about me." He felt his heart race.

"Sophia, we need you," Sarah called behind them.

Sophia looked back. "Yes, Sarah, coming." She turned to Clayton. "I guess I'd better get to work. Maybe we can talk more tomorrow."

Clayton nodded, then watched as she left the room. A few cards drifted to the floor, but he barely noticed. He'd forgotten why he had come.

seven

A white linen tablecloth stretched across the thick mahogany table, where a delicate centerpiece of candles and crystal adorned the middle. Sophia took a deep breath of the aromas wafting over the dinner table.

"Lord, we're very thankful for what You've placed before us this evening, and we give You praise for it. May we be ever mindful of Your goodness and always be ready to share," Mrs. Baird prayed. Mammá and Sophia joined in with whispered "Amens."

Seconds later, silverware clanged against the china as the bountiful bowls made their way around the table. For a few minutes, the trio said little, giving their full attention to the meal.

Mrs. Baird closed her eyes as she chewed a piece of roasted venison. She swallowed, then took a drink of water. "Angelica, I don't know where you learned to cook like this, but it's wonderful."

Mammá blushed from the compliment.

"My previous helper did a fine job for me, and I hated to see her move after the fire, but her cooking didn't compare to yours." Mrs. Baird lifted another bite to her mouth. "Thank you for helping this way." A quick smile touched her lips before she bit into another mouthful.

"Mrs. Baird, my friend, I could not stay here and take advantage of your kindness without doing my part. You deserve the thanks. Sophia and I would be on the street, if not for you."

Sophia nodded in agreement while eating boiled potatoes.

Mrs. Baird shifted and looked straight at Mammá. "Angelica,

there's something I want to ask you. You don't have to answer now, but I want you to think about it."

Mammá and Sophia looked at her.

"I know you've been searching for another boardinghouse." She leaned up to the table. "But I wonder if you would consider"—the older woman licked her lower lip—"um, consider living here as my friend?" As if remembering Mammá's proud spirit, she hurried to add, "You would still be cooking, of course, to earn your keep; but it would help me too. This big old house can get pretty lonely."

Sophia looked at her mother. Mammá stared across the table for a full minute before finding her voice. Tears swelled in her eyes. "Mrs. Baird, you are an answer to my prayers. I have feared the boarding business was becoming too much for me."

Mrs. Baird settled back into her chair with a thump of relief. Clasping shaking hands together, she said, "Good!"

For the next hour, they talked around the dinner table. After the meal, they went for tea in the sitting room. Mrs. Baird and Sophia settled into their comfortable seats. Mammá brought in a pot of brewed tea and poured the steaming hot liquid into their china cups. She gave a quick nod toward her friend.

Mrs. Baird turned to Sophia. "I know you have worked for several years creating fashionable dresses for the ladies in our town, Sophia. I've seen your work, and it is quite exquisite."

"Thank you, Mrs. Baird. Have I left too much of a mess in my room?" asked Sophia, worried the sewing clutter caused a problem.

"Oh, no, my dear." Mrs. Baird scooped some sugar into her tea and stirred, causing a light tinkling to fill the silence.

Sophia waited, wondering what was on Mrs. Baird's mind.

"I have a business proposition for you." Mrs. Baird took a sip of her tea, then peered over the rim of her cup.

"Oh?"

Mrs. Baird dabbed a napkin against her lips. "Yes, you see, I have a friend, Mr. Medill, and he's an established businessman in the railroad industry. I believe I've mentioned him to you?"

Sophia searched through her memory, but before she could answer, Mrs. Baird hurried on.

"Anyway, he grew up in Chicago, came from a poor home, and climbed his way up the ladder to success, thanks to an old gentleman who took an interest in Mr. Medill's ambitions." She took another sip from her cup before continuing. "The man has a soft spot in his heart for young people who work hard and need help getting started."

Sophia had no idea what all this had to do with her. She looked over at her mother, who was smiling. Something told Sophia the two of them were up to something. . .again.

"He's looking to invest in a business, and I told him about you and what a great seamstress you are, and—"

Sophia looked at her in disbelief.

"To shorten a terribly long story, he has purchased a little shop from a seamstress in town. She lost her husband a few months ago, so she's moving east to live with her daughter. He figured he'd offer you a building in which to run your business, and you, in turn, could provide him with a small rent. He will not burden you. The cost of the building is of no consequence to him. He simply offers you a dream-come-true, as someone once did for him, and you need only accept. One more thing: I've arranged with Mrs. Adams for you to receive a sewing machine of your own." Mrs. Baird flashed another of her triumphant smiles.

Sophia sat speechless. She knew Mrs. Baird had connections, but she never dreamed. . .

"What do you think?"

Mammá spoke up. "*Cara Mia,* are you all right?"

Excitement surged through Sophia. "You can't be serious."

"Oh, I'm serious, all right," Mrs. Baird said as she settled farther into her rocker, grinning with delight. "I'd like to take you there tomorrow."

Sophia had never had anything handed to her in all her life.

Her parents provided as best they could, but day-to-day living was a struggle as they worked to put food on the table. She hadn't minded doing without things because love abounded in their home. But her wildest imaginations could never have conjured up such a wonderful dream. She loved creating the latest fashions for women who appreciated them, and the thought of having her own machine, her own shop, made her head spin.

"But how could I repay him? I know nothing of running a business. How do I get started? Where will I find all the customers? Will I need people to help me?" Her words stumbled over each other in a torrent of questions, leaving her breathless.

Mrs. Baird stretched out an open palm. "Not to worry, my dear. First of all, with the customers you already have, I have complete confidence that you will make enough money to pay him back one day. But if you do not, it's a risk he's more than willing to take."

A log fell farther into the fire, scattering sparks about and distracting Mrs. Baird for a moment. She turned back to Sophia. "Mr. Medill has a nephew, Jonathan Clark, I believe it is, who just finished his schooling, with an expertise in business. Mr. Clark will manage some of Mr. Medill's rental properties as well as oversee your business. So you see, it's all arranged," Mrs. Baird said, but added in a hurry, "provided you agree, of course." Agnes Baird didn't blink as she waited for an answer.

Sophia looked to her mother for a sign. Mammá smiled. Turning her attention back to Mrs. Baird, Sophia replied, "How can I refuse?"

The two older women cheered and got up to hug her. The excited trio filled the sitting room with chatter, and Sophia realized in no time at all the three of them had imagined her new shop complete with furnishings, decorations, and customers standing in line.

❧

Sophia held the pin in her mouth as she worked the material

for the curtains, then fastened the cloth in place. "There. That should do it."

She looked up to see Mrs. Baird leafing through decorating books and Mammá busy writing.

"Are you still making a list of food items needed for the Thanksgiving dinner, Mammá?"

For a moment, her mother didn't answer. "What? Oh, yes, I'm sorry. I don't want to forget anything. If I know our friend, she'll invite extra guests who have no place to go to our feast." Mammá looked at Mrs. Baird and smiled.

Mrs. Baird shrugged. "Can't have people being alone on a special day."

The room grew quiet for awhile.

"You know, I really like the name we picked out for the shop," Sophia said, breaking the silence. "The Thread Bearer." She rolled the words around on her tongue. "Yes, I like it," she announced with a sharp nod of her head.

They all agreed.

The following days, Sophia worked hard to prepare her shop for opening. She polished the place until it shone and finished making the light blue, ruffled curtains for the front room, while hired hands whitewashed the walls around her. Mrs. Baird consulted with Sophia. Then, at her own expense, the older woman flitted about town ordering appropriate furnishings, decorations, and such, making sure everything was perfect. When Sophia tried to protest, Mrs. Baird indicated she would be more than recompensed when she appeared in one of Sophia's beautiful creations.

Friday afternoon, Mrs. Baird, Mammá, and Sophia stood in the entrance and marveled at the quaint little place, clean with the smell of a good whitewashing. Sophia had to pinch herself to make sure she wasn't caught up in a beautiful dream.

A glowing lantern stood on a round, chintz-covered oak table situated in the corner of the small waiting room. On either side of the table stood small cushioned chairs with soft, fluffy pillows resting at their backs. Deeper into the room, Sophia's sewing area was hidden from view by a large, wooden partition. Customers could see the tip of her head as they entered, but the clutter of the sewing machine and fragments of material were out of sight.

In the middle of the room, to the left of the sewing area, a small counter guarded a backdrop of shelves stacked in a neat fashion with bolts of colored cloth, laces, buttons, threads, and ribbons.

A small, arched entryway led into a back room with a cozy kitchen. To the left, a thick blue curtain separated the dressing area from the kitchen. Before the curtain, a full-length looking glass hung from the wall for convenience in final fittings.

A jangling gold bell over the front door completed the project.

Sophia turned to her mother and Mrs. Baird. "Isn't it beautiful?"

The grinning duo agreed. They stepped into the room, inspecting each nook and cranny to make sure Sophia had things the way she wanted them.

"Before he leaves for New York, Mr. Medill will be by this afternoon with his nephew to talk to you again."

Sophia turned to Mrs. Baird. "He's such a nice man. I can't believe he did this for me. And I can't believe you talked him into it." She poked her in a playful manner.

The older woman waved her hand. "Glad to help. Besides, I'm looking forward to that new dress!"

"Done," Sophia returned. She glanced at the shelf clock. "Oh, I must be going. I promised Mrs. Adams I would come back to the Relief Center this afternoon and finish some paperwork."

"*Cara Mia,* are you sure you can continue to work there while running your shop?" Mammá gave Sophia a worried look.

"I'll be fine. I'm only helping out from time to time. My

business isn't exactly booming just yet." She laughed.

"Oh, don't you worry about that, young lady. As soon as the word gets out that you have a shop, you'll have more work than you could imagine." Mrs. Baird looked around the room. "Yes, indeed."

"Just don't work yourself too hard," Mammá said, giving Sophia a look of motherly concern. "I guess we'd better be going too. I've got a chicken to prepare for dinner." Mammá ran her fingers one last time over the curtains and shook her head. "So lovely, Sophia."

The three stepped through the door, and Sophia turned to pull it shut, taking one last glimpse around the room. She sighed with pleasure, then tugged the locked door closed, listening to the light tinkling of the bell. She still felt she had stepped into a dream. Perhaps she had.

eight

A gust of November wind swirled colored leaves through the air, brushing them lightly against the windowpane. Clayton looked up from the real estate issues on which he worked and glanced at the gloomy sky.

Exhaling a weary breath, he rubbed his tired eyes and sat back in his chair, scanning the room. Law books lined the opposite wall, client chairs perched just beyond his desk, and a grandfather clock stood in the corner, bonging the hour. A wooden rack, laden with his coat and scarf, reminded him winter was just around the corner.

He glanced again at his desk cluttered with open books, miscellaneous documents, and letters. He closed his eyes to the disorder and stretched. A deep yawn followed. Since his sickness, he found himself tiring easily. His ambitions attempted to carry him further than his strength allowed. The doctor encouraged him to ease back into a normal life rather than plunging in all at once. Clayton was beginning to see the wisdom of the doctor's advice.

Clayton snapped shut the law book and, with some effort, rose to his feet.

"Dad, I think I'm going to leave. I'm pretty tired," said Clayton upon entering his father's office.

His dad stopped reading and looked up. "All right. Tell Mother I'll be home around seven o'clock."

"I'll let her know." Clayton pushed open the door and pulled his coat closer to ward off the cold air. He squinted against the stinging wind. With a quick tug, he yanked the brim of his hat over his eyes to keep out the elements. He walked over to the hitching post in front of the office. His legs ached as he

56

climbed into the carriage. The horses trotted steadily down the road, allowing Clayton to view the rebuilding of the city and mull over the past weeks.

At last, he drew to a stop in front of Lincoln Park. The homeless crowd had dwindled, thanks to the new shanties springing up.

Clayton tethered his horses and walked through the park. Forgotten debris and discarded fire pits littered the area. The remaining people moved wearily through their evening routine, faces drawn with hopelessness, their clothes tattered and dirty, drooping on their thinning bodies.

He stopped at a campsite. "Excuse me. I'm looking for a young lady and her mother."

Bent over a campfire, the old woman extended a long, thin tree branch to turn a log on the ground. It sent tiny sparks swirling. Her lifeless eyes turned to meet him. Dirt lined the creases in her face. Weighted words revealed the heavy load she carried. "What are their names?"

He cleared his throat. "Uh, well, I don't know their names."

"What do they look like?" A cold gust of wind blew in their direction. With gnarled fingers, she pulled her tattered shawl tight around her wrinkled neck.

Clayton began to feel foolish. "I'm not really sure what they look like, but I thought maybe if you had seen two women—"

Impatience twisted her face. "Are you serious? Do you know how many people have been in and out of here?" She turned her head and gestured for him to go away.

"Sorry to trouble you, Ma'am." Clayton reached for her hand and pressed some money into her palm.

An expression mixed with surprise and appreciation crossed her face. Clayton tipped his hat and turned away.

He walked past the remaining campsites, glanced at the tired faces, and decided not to ask any more questions. He realized his search was futile. Shoulders slumped, he climbed back into his rig, feeling more tired than ever. The horses turned toward home. Clayton felt low in spirit. He would give up his search for now.

After dinner, Clayton retired early. Once inside his room, he pulled out the journal again.

December 15. The whole city is dressed in white today! How I love a freshly fallen snow.

Clayton smiled as he read the words. He felt the same way. How many times had he and his friends romped in the snow, creating fortresses and shelters in which to hide from flying snowballs? The childhood memory made him feel warm and cold all at the same time.

Mammá and I called on a friend from church tonight, and as we traveled through the winding country roads, we saw some young people riding on a sleigh, laughing and having a wonderful time. I would love to go on a sleigh ride! I imagined I was on the ride with them, feeling the dusty puffs of blowing snow press cold against my skin, tiny snowflakes fluttering upon my wet lashes, hearing the quiet jingle of bells, snuggling under warm buffalo skins, and gliding happily through the country. I know I shouldn't talk like that. Mammá would not be pleased. Still, I can't help myself. One day I shall ride in a sleigh.

Once again, the words in the journal warmed him. This woman's writings had a way of making him feel better, lighter, at the end of a long day. His eyelids drooped. He would read more tomorrow. For now, he placed the secret writings back into the trunk.

With a quick exhalation, he snuffed out the lantern's light. The soft bed creaked slightly as he settled into the crisp linens.

In no time at all, he drifted into a dream filled with a sleigh, falling snow, and a faceless woman beside him.

❧

"Isn't winter wonderful!" Sophia exclaimed breathlessly as she shook snow off the arms of her cloak. She'd come through the "employees only" entrance of the Relief Center. Some workers looked at her in agreement, others groaned. Clayton watched her with interest. A soft crimson colored her face, cooled by the brisk air.

Sophia pulled off her wraps while looking at her new friends. "What, doesn't anyone around here enjoy the season's first snowfall?" No one answered. Most shook their heads, but Sophia didn't seem to notice. She hung her dark cloak on a peg, peeked out the window, and sighed.

Clayton came up behind her and whispered, "I like it."

Sophia turned to face him. They stood so close, Clayton could feel her breath against his face. She gasped and turned back toward the window.

"I'm sorry, I didn't mean to startle you." Clayton moved to her side and watched the snowflakes flutter upon the windowpane.

He peered at Sophia. She stood transfixed by the frosty, white air, and he stood transfixed by her. A tinge of pink touched the tip of her nose, and she smelled as fresh as new-fallen snow. Not wanting to embarrass her, he forced himself to look away from her and back toward the winter scene before them. His thoughts drifted to the journal, and it surprised him. The journal writer liked winter too. Perhaps that's why he thought of her. He shrugged off his musings.

An idea struck him. "Do you like sleigh rides?"

Sophia turned sparkling eyes toward him. "Doesn't everybody?"

"Believe it or not, there are people in this world who do not enjoy a good sleigh ride. I take it you're not one of them?"

Sophia bit her lip and shook her head.

Her enthusiasm encouraged him. "Maybe we could go on a sleigh ride sometime?" He searched her face.

"I would love to go on a sleigh ride," she exclaimed with as much excitement as befit a young lady.

"Time to take your posts, please," Mrs. Adams's voice croaked to the volunteers.

Clayton grabbed Sophia's hand and gave it a quick squeeze. "We'll talk later."

Workers scrambled to their places as Mrs. Adams went to open the doors for a new day.

❧

Sophia had just settled into her seat and thought about how thankful she was that her work at The Thread Bearer hadn't consumed her yet so she had time to help out at the Relief Center. Even though she wouldn't admit it, she was happier still for excuses to see Clayton.

A young blond woman walked up, holding hands with two miniature replicas of herself. Sophia assumed they were this woman's daughters. The youngest one looked to be about three years old. She peeked around the folds of her mother's skirt. Sophia gave her a gentle smile, and the girl snuggled closer to her mother, all the while watching Sophia.

"May I help you?" Sophia asked.

The woman swallowed, her eyes filled with worry. She began in a whisper. "My husband is sick. I didn't know where to go. We. . .we have no food." She lowered her head.

Sophia felt compassion swell within her. It seemed the woman didn't want to ask for help, unlike the many others who came in asking for free handouts with no regard for the less fortunate.

"Where is your husband now, Ma'am?" Sophia asked in a soft voice.

"He is in our shanty." Bright tears formed in her eyes. "I am worried."

"What is your name, please?"

"Marie Zimmerman." She turned to the little girls beside her and tapped each one on the head as she announced, "These are my daughters, Elizabeth and Abigail."

"Hello, Elizabeth, Abigail," Sophia said in a voice she hoped would put them at ease. "My name is Sophia Martone."

"My husband has been working hard at odd jobs, trying to put food on our table. He is a proud man and refuses to ask for help. He would not like me being here, but he is so sick." Her eyes pleaded for understanding. "I had to come."

"You did the right thing, Mrs. Zimmerman."

The woman lifted her head. "Thank you. Please call me Marie."

Sophia nodded. She quickly jotted their names on paper, then stood. "Follow me, please."

The little family followed Sophia as she took them to the doctor's table and explained the situation. He said he would take a look at her husband in the afternoon, as soon as he finished giving out vaccinations.

Sophia then led them to a room where workers distributed food. Satisfied the family received the help they needed, she walked them to the front door.

Marie turned before leaving. "Miss, could you come with the doctor?"

The request filled Sophia with tenderness. "Of course, Marie. I would be happy to come."

Marie gave a simple nod of appreciation.

Sophia bent down to look at the girls. "Everything will be all right." She gently patted each one on the arm. A hint of trust flickered in their eyes.

They said their good-byes, and Sophia whispered a prayer for them. She remembered her own feelings when her father had become ill. Her heart warmed to this family. She wanted to help them in any way possible.

❧

Later in the afternoon, Dr. Ollis and Sophia pulled up to a street

lined with shanties. They drew to a stop in front of the
Zimmermans' home. The little cottage was about twenty by
sixteen, which Sophia remembered was the size allowed by the
Relief Center to a family of three or more. Once they entered
the home, Sophia observed felt lining on the inside walls, a
double iron chimney, three windows covered with simple
beige curtains, and a partition dividing two bedrooms from
the living area. Used furniture decorated the room, and a
small woodstove offered warmth. Though the Zimmermans
owned few possessions, everything sparkled. Sophia could
sense love within their home the moment she entered.

The doctor went into one of the bedrooms to check Seth
Zimmerman, while Sophia talked with Marie, Elizabeth, and
Abigail.

The little girls began to open up to Sophia, showing her
their dolls. The cloth dolls were frayed and soiled from endless hours of hugs and playing. Sophia expressed her praise
of each doll, then handed them back to the girls.

The doctor came over to Marie and Sophia. "He has overworked himself and will only get worse if he doesn't rest.
You will see that he stays in bed?"

"Yes," Mrs. Zimmerman answered, looking through the
open doorway at her husband.

"I trust you are boiling your water?" the doctor asked, raising a concerned brow.

"Yes, Doctor."

"Good." He pulled on his hat. "I question the water's
safety, even now. There are still cases of smallpox, cholera,
and typhoid fever out there. We've got to take precautions,"
he said as one with authority. "I'm glad you were able to get
a stove. Some weren't so lucky."

"Yes, Sir. We are blessed."

"Is there any work you can take in, Mrs. Zimmerman?" Dr.
Ollis asked.

She thought for a minute. "I do some sewing, but I don't

know where to go—"

Before she could finish, Sophia interrupted her. "I sew dresses for ladies in town and could use a little help. I know you qualify for a sewing machine. Maybe you could assist me."

Marie's eyes brightened with hope. "I would work hard, Sophia." She grabbed Sophia's hands.

"I know you would, Marie. I'll go through my things tonight and stop by tomorrow afternoon. I'll have someone bring the machine over in the morning, then I'll visit in the afternoon to teach you how to operate it."

"Oh, thank you." Marie hugged her. "Seth told me God would make a way. Why do I worry?"

Sophia understood. She, too, struggled to trust God during the hard times.

Waving good-bye, Sophia joined the doctor in the carriage, and they headed back to the center.

nine

"I'll only be gone a couple of hours, Mrs. Adams," Sophia said, reaching for her cloak. "Besides, Mr. Higgins will be here at five o'clock, and I don't want to keep him waiting in the cold."

Mrs. Adams shook her head and clicked her tongue. "You should not go unescorted, Sophia. It's not proper." Her mouth pulled tight with disapproval.

Sophia smiled sweetly. *Dear Mrs. Adams. She looks after her workers like a hen over her chicks.*

Sophia tried to follow the rules of propriety for the most part, but she stubbornly drew a line when it interfered with helping another. "I will be fine, really." She reached over to Mrs. Adams and gave her a reassuring hug.

Walking over to the table, Sophia lifted a paper bearing the Zimmermans' address and folded it neatly in half. Although she had been there with Dr. Ollis, the shanties looked similar, and being alone, she didn't want to approach the wrong one.

She glanced back at Mrs. Adams. "I'll be back soon. It's not too far." Sophia wrapped her neck in a woolen scarf and eased on her gloves.

"You're sure it's not too far to walk? I'll be glad to take you," offered Mrs. Adams, her forehead creased with concern.

"The walk will do me good. I need the fresh air." Sophia waved good-bye before exiting the door.

The air did feel good, she decided as she walked through the snowy streets of Chicago. Sitting at her post in the center made her sleepy in the afternoons. This brisk walk would certainly wake her up. A sudden gust of wind raced past her, causing Sophia to pull her scarf closer to her face. She inhaled a quick, shivering breath, feeling invigorated by the season's winds.

Her thoughts drifted to Clayton. She was surprised he had asked her to go on a sleigh ride. Of course, they hadn't set an actual date. He suggested that maybe they could go sometime. She sighed, her boot kicking a chunk of snow from her path. But why did he squeeze her hand? He seemed to have some interest in her. Sophia felt her cheeks heat and chided herself for thinking such bold thoughts.

She shook off her mental wanderings and looked around her. Recognizing the street lined with shanties, she moved forward in search of the Zimmermans' home. A few men stood outside their shacks, apparently with nothing to do but watch people passing by. Sophia felt uncomfortable with the way they looked at her and hurried on until she came to the Zimmermans' shanty.

Marie answered the door. "Sophia, please come in."

Warmth touched her stinging cheeks the moment she entered. The room smelled of simmering stew. Elizabeth and Abigail played quietly with their dolls in a corner of the room. They both got up when they saw Sophia enter and shyly walked over to greet her.

"Girls, let Miss Sophia pull off her wraps before you bother her."

"No bother at all." Sophia shifted out of her coverings, then stooped to say hello. The children offered news about their day before Marie kindly told them to go back to their dolls.

Sophia hadn't even noticed Marie's husband sitting up in a wooden chair by the potbellied stove. "Sophia, this is my husband, Seth."

She walked over to him and observed that it took a great deal of effort for him to rise.

He tipped his head. "I understand we are beholden to you, Miss Martone."

"Please call me Sophia. We haven't done much really, but I'm glad we could be of some help." He looked like it took everything in him to hold himself up.

"We're beholden to you, just the same."

Sophia noticed even in his weakened condition he stood a head taller than she. His pale skin stretched tight across his gaunt form. Dark shadows underlined the sunken, faded eyes that greeted her, and Sophia thought he looked as though he'd been on a lengthy fast. Settling gently back into his chair, Seth Zimmerman let out an involuntary sigh.

Marie stirred the pot of stew, sending the aroma of beef and vegetables around the room, then turned to Sophia. "I have the machine on the table." Her voice sounded like that of a child about to receive a special surprise. Beside the machine were items Marie had made by hand. She passed them to Sophia for her inspection. Sophia looked them over with interest. She ran her hands over the smooth seams, carefully observing the stitching.

"These are very good, Marie," Sophia said, looking up from the material. "It will be wonderful to have you helping me."

Relief seemed to wash over Marie. The two sat down at the table, and Sophia began to go over different aspects of the machine. Finally, when Sophia felt confident Marie knew how to operate it, she rose to leave.

"You must stay and have stew with us," Marie insisted. "O'Connell's Grocery Store is giving out free meat. We would love to share our good fortune with you."

Sophia started to decline but, looking at Marie, thought better of it. These people had pride. The stew would be their way of giving back. "Thank you," she heard herself saying.

Elizabeth and Abigail gathered handmade wooden bowls and placed them on the rough pine table. In the center, a kerosene lamp cast a warm glow across the faces surrounding the table.

The little family bowed their heads and closed their eyes.

Sophia did the same.

"Dear Lord," Mr. Zimmerman began, "we thank You for this wonderful dinner. Many of our neighbors go to bed without food tonight. Help us to share and be thankful for what we have. We thank You, too, for Sophia and the Relief Center helping us get back on our feet. You always take care of us, Father, and we are grateful. In Jesus' Name, amen."

In no time, the little group emptied the stew from the pot, enjoying comfortable fellowship all the while. Sophia helped clear the table and thanked her hostess and family for their kindness. She had no idea how long she had been in their home but felt sure it was getting close to five o'clock. *Oh, why didn't I bring my timepiece with me?*

When she stepped outside, panic stirred within her. The dark streets told her Mr. Higgins had waited far too long for her at the Relief Center. No doubt, he would be worried. The street lamps offered little comfort as they flickered upon the quiet streets.

She stepped forward at a quickened pace, crunching snow beneath her feet. The deafening stillness on the road chilled her more than the frigid air. Her senses sharpened. A dog barked from a distant home, causing her to jump. She felt foolish.

"You shouldn't go out unescorted, Sophia." Mrs. Adams's words played upon her mind, growing stronger with the howling wind that clawed at her cloak. She lifted her chin and squared her shoulders, forcing herself to remain calm.

Looking toward the shanties, she watched as smoke spiraled from the chimneys. She assumed everyone was gathering for dinner. The thought of family and mealtime caused her body to relax a little. Still, she walked at a steady pace and focused on getting back to the center before everyone worried about her.

Suddenly, a large man dressed in ragged clothes stepped through the shadows, blocking Sophia's path. His intentions were clear. Terror seared through Sophia's body like a hot iron. A short gasp lodged in her throat as fear silenced her screams. Her pulse drummed staccato beats hard against her temple, making her feel like a frightened rabbit. With frantic eyes, she searched the deserted streets for help. A chill as cold as death settled upon her.

The man let out a low laugh. "Well, now, what have we here?" His icy voice cut through her skin like a hunter's knife on its prey. Sophia felt paralyzed for a moment.

"Excuse me, Sir, but someone is waiting for me." She tried to calm her quivering voice.

The man grabbed her arm. "Is that right?"

Sophia jerked her hand, trying to squirm loose while he looked behind him.

He turned back to face her. "Aw, ain't it a shame?" he taunted, "I guess he ain't here yet, little miss."

Bursts of cheap whiskey soiled every word, bringing back a forgotten memory of her papá throwing out a drunken boarder from their home long ago. The street lamps revealed red, bloodshot eyes. But something else lurked within them. What? His slimy teeth showed traces of tobacco juice as his mouth twisted in an eager sneer.

Nausea crawled up Sophia's throat as the man bent his head toward her. She cried through a cracked whisper, "Dear God, please help me."

❧

Clayton tugged on his hat as he walked down the steps of the center, surprised to see Sophia's driver. "Hello, Higgins. You're still waiting for Sophia?"

"Yes, Sir. I've been out here for about forty-five minutes now. It's not like her to be this late."

Clayton could see worry in the old driver's eyes. "I'll check in the center for you. Be back in a minute." He leapt up the stairs, taking two at a time. Pushing through the doors, he caught Mrs. Adams just as she was leaving.

"Mrs. Adams, is Sophia still here?"

She looked up with a start. "Why, no, Clayton. I'm the last one. I was just getting ready to lock up."

Panic fringed the edge of his mind, but Clayton shoved it away. "Her driver is here. She must not have gone home, or he would know it."

"Oh, dear."

"What is it?" Clayton asked with more calm than he felt.

"She went to the Zimmermans' home today, and come to think of it, I don't think she came back. I told her not to go alone." The old woman shook her head with dismay.

"Where do they live?" Fear pricked his spine.

Mrs. Adams thought for a minute. "The application. The address would be on Mrs. Zimmerman's application for a sewing machine."

They ran into the room where Sophia worked, and Mrs. Adams pulled out a file of forms. Rummaging quickly through them, she finally lifted Mrs. Zimmerman's application from the stack.

"Here it is." She raised her bony arm and waved the application.

Clayton cast a hasty glance at the paper, then ran out the door, yelling, "Thank you."

Racing down the steps, he called to Mr. Higgins. "Go on home. I know where Sophia is, and I will bring her home."

"Is she all right?"

"She's fine," Clayton said, praying it was true.

With a quick flip of the reins, he took his horses through the streets, fear guiding him all the way. He knew the area where the shanties stood. Some rough characters lived there, and he wasn't about to take any chances on Sophia getting hurt.

❧

"Ain't no use tryin' to get away, little miss. I got myself a reputation around here. Ain't nobody gonna try to stop me."

Sophia continued to squirm, trying to pull away. He scratched his rough face against hers. His whiskers raked hard over her cheek. She pulled her leg back and kicked him with all the force she could muster. He winced but seemed to enjoy the struggle. He acted as though her spirit offered more of a challenge to him. He threw his head back in a wicked laugh and pulled her closer.

Tightening his grip on her wrists, his smile twisted into an angry leer. His black eyes formed narrow slits. "No use fightin' me." He ground his words through clenched teeth. His deep voice filled her with doom. "This night, you belong to me."

Horror punched her hard, deep in the pit of her stomach. She ached as if she had just been run over by a carriage. She tried to scream, but her attempts were weak. Right then, the man's thick, filthy hand clamped firmly across her mouth, smothering her cries. She struggled to breathe. Her body recoiled and thrashed against him, but his strength overpowered her. Only muffled whimpers escaped through the slits between his fingers.

"Stop right there." The words were spoken with strength and command.

Startled, the man turned to see who would dare confront him. Sophia's eyes grew wide upon seeing Clayton. Her cries caught in her throat.

"And who's going to stop me?"

"Look, just let her go. You're drunk. I don't want to hurt you."

A mixture of fear and admiration washed over her for Clayton. Sophia felt the man's foul breath against her face as he made a low, guttural growl. He dropped her behind him like a rag doll.

With a thud, she fell into the snow, too paralyzed to move.

"*You* don't want to hurt *me?*" He roared as if someone had just told a crusty joke. The laughing came to an abrupt halt. Thick fingers rolled up his sleeves, and the man began to sway like an experienced fighter.

"Sophia, get in my carriage," Clayton commanded without ever looking at her.

She couldn't move. Fear had turned her arms and legs to stone. She willed them to action, but they wouldn't budge.

"If you want to get the little lady, you're going to have to go through me first," the man sneered, spitting tobacco juice at Clayton.

"Look, Mister, just leave her alone. Go home and sleep it off."

Sophia watched as the street lamp lit upon Clayton's face, revealing his tense jaws and flashing, dark eyes. She could see his lips move faintly and wondered if he was praying for the strength to keep his anger under control.

The drunkard pulled his arm back to take a swing, but the whiskey slowed his actions. Clayton ducked to miss the punch. The man wobbled, trying to regain his balance. Clayton attempted to get to Sophia, but the man doubled his fist and took another swing. This time, Clayton rolled to the ground. The man's force made him circle twice and fall flat to the hard, snowy earth.

Clayton could have pounded the man good but instead just looked at him. Sophia held her breath, praying Clayton would not strike back. She wanted to get out of there as quickly as possible. Fighting the man wouldn't solve anything. She prayed God would give Clayton the wisdom and strength to leave well enough alone.

He did.

Calm coursed through her.

The man tried to lift himself from the snow, but the effort proved too much, and he dropped his head back, surrendering to the drunken sleep that claimed him.

By now, the neighbors had come out of their homes and surrounded them.

"It's Jake Elders," one called out. The others mumbled among themselves.

"That good-for-nothing—"

A woman of slight build approached them. Her face was pale as muslin. A large, purplish bruise flamed from her right cheek. She nervously licked her lips as she looked from Sophia to Clayton. She bent down in the snow and felt Jake's pulse. Sad eyes looked toward Sophia. "He didn't mean no harm, Ma'am. It's the drink. It always does this to him." The woman absently reached up to touch her bruise.

Sophia just looked at her, too shaken to speak.

"Come on, Sadie. I'll help you get him in the house," her neighbor said. The man helped Sadie pull Jake back toward their house, and the people began to return to their homes.

Clayton looked over at Sophia. "Are you all right?" He inched closer to her.

Shaking uncontrollably, she leaned into his arms and cried more tears than she knew she had in her.

As the crowd parted, Mr. Higgins's voice called from behind, startling them both. "Miss Sophia, might I take you home?"

Clayton looked at him with surprise.

"Beg your pardon, Sir, but when I saw the worry on your face, I had to follow you and make sure Miss Sophia was all right."

Although disappointed he wouldn't be taking Sophia home, Clayton understood the driver's concern.

Sophia nodded, wiped her eyes, and rose to her feet. "Thank you, Clayton," she whispered before turning to go with Mr. Higgins.

ten

The next morning, tiny snowflakes drifted past Sophia's windowpane. She rubbed her sleepy eyes and glanced at them. Stubborn sunlight pushed through the dainty sheers and spilled gently into the room. Sophia stretched and yawned. What time was it, anyhow?

Reluctantly, her feet hit the rug, and she stood, pulling on her robe and slippers, compliments of Mrs. Baird. With a contented gaze outside, she looked onto the snow-covered wonderland and sighed. The town looked clean, the air clear as a sparkling crystal glass. She leaned against the frame and enjoyed the moment until thoughts of the evening before intruded her peaceful musings.

"What a horrible man," she muttered with a shiver, drawing the warm robe closer. She turned from the window and walked to the dresser. As she settled into a wooden chair, she reached for a hairbrush, then pulled it thoughtfully through her hair.

She felt thankful for Clayton's timely arrival the night before. Who knew what might have happened if he hadn't come? Goosebumps appeared on her arms, and she rubbed them vigorously. She would not think about Jake Elders. The mere thought of his name constricted her breathing. She must forget the whole incident.

A picture of Clayton's protective stance flashed across her thoughts. He stood tall, confident, determined. Never had he looked so handsome. Her heart gave a light flutter.

"He rescued me." The words lingered in the air.

Suddenly the thought of Mr. Higgins showing up to take her home jolted through her. If the driver hadn't shown up,

Clayton would have driven her home and discovered she lived with Mrs. Baird. Sophia determined she had to be more careful, for more reasons than her safety.

Pulling herself from her daydreams, she bent over, twisted her hair, then lifted upright and twirled it into a knot on the back of her head. Tucking ends here and there with hairpins, she cast one last glance in the looking glass. She shrugged on a simple frock and, finally satisfied she was presentable for breakfast, made her way down the stairs.

Mrs. Baird hadn't heard of Sophia's confrontation. Between bites of sausage and biscuits, Sophia explained what had happened. Mrs. Baird and Mammá talked about the dangers of the present world and how unsafe it seemed for a woman to go out of the house these days, while Sophia allowed her thoughts to drift to Clayton once again. She remembered how he kept his arm around her after the ordeal and let her cry, drawing her protectively close to him. It felt wonderful to her then and even now, as she relived the moment.

When Sophia excused herself from the table, she went to her room to wash and prepare for the day. She felt grateful to have Saturday afternoon free from work. With Marie's sewing help, Sophia would have a little more free time. Though the Martones needed the money, Sophia was thankful to have enough work to help the Zimmerman family get through this difficult time. She had to admit it also helped allow her to volunteer at the Relief Center.

Later that afternoon, Mr. Higgins drew the carriage to a stop in front of the house. Sophia climbed aboard. She wondered if this could be the day she would find their trunk. Her thoughts barely had time to surface before they arrived at their destination.

Sophia climbed out. A quick gust of wind caused her to hold her scarf in place just under her chin. "Thank you, Mr. Higgins. I shouldn't be long. Are you sure you'll be all right, waiting in the cold?"

"I'll be fine, Ma'am," he returned, huddling deeper into his coat. "Take your time."

The winter sun teased them with warmth, peeking in and out of the swelling gray clouds. Sophia glanced at the sky. "Looks like it might snow again." She bit her lip and looked at Mr. Higgins. "You sure you'll be all right?"

He tipped the brim of his hat with gloved fingers. "I'll be fine." He patted the seat beside him, revealing a copy of the *Chicago Tribune* to keep him occupied.

Indecision plagued her as she walked toward the old brick building. She wondered if she should leave poor Mr. Higgins to wait in the cold. Glancing back, she found him already happily lost in the day's news.

Satisfied, Sophia lifted her skirt hastily and continued toward the warehouse door. Her thoughts went to Mrs. Baird. Sophia felt blessed to have her as a friend. The woman had more friends than Sophia could count.

Sophia had told Mrs. Baird about the family trunk. The very next day, the dear woman came home breathless with excitement, telling Sophia of the old warehouse on Elm Street and the possibility of the trunk being stored there. Then she proudly pulled a shiny key from her pocket and handed it to Sophia. "This will get you in," she had said.

Sophia shook her head with the memory. *Dear Mrs. Baird, always looking out for others.*

After pushing in the key, Sophia opened the door. She felt unprepared for the site. Enormous piles of unclaimed family possessions of every shape, size, and color were strewn about haphazardly.

She stood overwhelmed for a moment, taking it all in, then went back outside to explain to Mr. Higgins he could come back in an hour to pick her up. It would take her at least that long to search through the surface rubble. He offered to help her, but she refused. He wouldn't recognize it, and she really preferred this time to herself. He would wait at a nearby restaurant and enjoy some coffee.

Sophia stepped back into the warehouse. With determination, she lifted her chin and rolled up her sleeves. "No use fretting about it. I might as well start looking," she mumbled, as she began to sort through the clutter.

❧

"Still no luck with the trunk, Sophia?" Mrs. Baird asked as the three took their seats in the sitting room for their usual evening chat.

Sophia shook her head sadly.

"I'm afraid we have lost it forever." Sorrow underlined Mammá's words.

"Never say never. There's always hope," Mrs. Baird said before taking a drink of tea.

The more Sophia got to know Mrs. Baird, the more she loved the woman. Her contagious, optimistic attitude often carried Sophia and her mother through their discouragement. In a way, Mrs. Baird reminded Sophia of her papá, who also saw the world through positive eyes.

"I guess money is coming in from all over the country to help our city." Mrs. Baird moved rhythmically in her rocking chair. "It's good to know there are still caring people in this world."

"I'm sure it takes a little of the burden from Mayor Mason's shoulders," Sophia added.

Mammá shook her head. "After the fire, they say a third of the city was homeless."

"I'm thankful the rainstorm came when it did. No doubt, it saved the city from much more destruction." Mrs. Baird tapped her teaspoon lightly against the rim of her cup and placed it on the saucer. "Sophia, I understand Clayton Hill is doing better?"

"Yes, he is." She could hear the relief in her own voice. Her eyes glanced at her mother, who was wearing a curious smile. Sophia wondered why.

&

"Why does Sophia have to be so beautiful?" Clayton asked himself in his room as he stared at the unopened journal. His hands felt clammy, a little shaky. Thoughts of Sophia's face, her dark compassionate eyes, held him still for a moment.

Grabbing the journal, he shook it as if an answer would fall from its pages. "Why do I care about you?" He sighed and placed the book on his nightstand. He began to pace.

Who am I trying to fool? I have feelings for Sophia. There's no use denying it. He took forceful steps across the floor. *I think she cares about me too.* Reaching the other wall, he turned and started pacing again.

He stopped in front of the stand and picked up the journal. "And then, there's you!" he said out loud, carrying the writings with him in his frustrated walk. "I don't even know you! Why can't I get you out of my mind?"

A knock sounded at the door. "Clayton, are you all right?"

He stopped abruptly. "Yes, Mom, I'm fine." His gaze fell upon a law book. He quickly picked it up and opened it to the marked page he had planned to study later that evening. "Uh, I'm going over a case I've got pending." He was too embarrassed to talk about his real dilemma.

A light laugh came through the door. "Oh, all right, Dear."

Her feet padded down the hall, and he took a deep breath to calm himself before settling on the bed. He glanced at the page in the law book. Rambled thoughts caused the words to blur. With a sigh, he closed the book and gazed absently at the ceiling.

Thoughts of Sophia being approached by Jake Elders caused anger to surge through him. "If he had hurt her in any way. . ." His whispered words trailed off. He shuddered to think what he would do if she were hurt. Remembering her frightened eyes and her trembling arms as he held her made him want to reach out to her even now. So vulnerable. So beautiful.

His gaze fell upon the journal in his hand.

"Why can't I just put this away and forget about it?" He waited, staring at the bound secrets of another. There were many pages still to be read. Something pulled him to it. What? His jaw tensed as he worked through his frustration.

Before he knew it, the fragile pages began to rustle lightly, and he started to read the next entry.

December 25. Such a delightful day! I awoke with the excitement of a child and hurried to the sitting room. The decorated tree stood in the corner, and as I had expected, there sat the special trunk, sealed tightly with a lock. Mammá was waiting with a smile, along with some of the boarders.

We all sat around the Christmas tree, sipping hot cider while Mammá read the Christmas story.

"So you see," she said in almost a whisper, "the manger held life's most precious Gift, wrapped in swaddling clothes. Jesus, God's only Son, came to share the good news of His Father's love for a lost world and to offer hope for everyone who believes."

I saw Mr. Beasley brush away a tear. Mammá asked me to say the prayer, which I was glad to do; then we sang Christmas carols. We had a grand time!

Mammá turned to me and threw me a wink before she opened the trunk. I felt all the wonderment of my childhood wash over me as I heard the familiar sound of Mammá jostling with the lock. My heart pounded hard.

She began to pull out presents one at a time. No one was forgotten. Mammá knit thick yarns into warm hats, scarves, and mittens. The boarders joined in, giving Mammá and me presents of caramels, walnuts, and oranges.

Mammá gave me a very lovely bonnet, one I wanted for a long time. I presented her with a dress I made for

her to wear to church. I thought we had a wonderful
Christmas. Then, when the boarders left and we were
alone, she called me over to the trunk. Then she pulled
out the most wonderful gift of all.

Mammá's eyes filled with tears as she passed the
treasured present to me. A delicate cloth held the item.
I opened it, and to my astonishment, there lay Papá's
Bible!

I cried and tried to protest, to tell Mammá it belonged
to her, but she would not listen. She told me Papá would
want me to have it.

He bought the Bible when we moved to America.
Reading it, we learned more about God, and we learned
how to speak better English. I remember night after
night when we would gather in the sitting room where
Papá would read the wonderful stories.

Mammá shared some of their favorite passages from
his Bible and told me why they had meant so much to
him. I felt closer to him than ever.

I miss Papá, and now that I have his Bible, I know I
shall always have him with me.

Clayton loved her sensitive nature, her passion for life and
for others. He knelt beside the trunk and pulled out the Bible
again. *This must be her father's Bible. "L." His name started*
with an "L." His finger slowly outlined the letter. Too bad he
couldn't read the last name.

This trunk and these belongings are valuable to this
daughter and her mother. If only I could find them.

eleven

"It's hard to believe we have so much snow even before Thanksgiving," Clayton said as he ran his fingers along the windowsill at the Relief Center, watching lacy flakes fall from the frosty sky.

Sophia eyed him curiously. His comment seemed to have a hidden meaning.

He turned to face her. "It's a perfect day for a sleigh ride. Want to go?"

Sophia's heart quickened. "You mean today?"

"Uh-huh." Amusement touched his face.

She nervously straightened her applications into tidy stacks, while her mind raced for an answer. He couldn't pick her up at Mrs. Baird's house, because he might know the older woman, and then he would know the home did not belong to Sophia's family. Oh, why had she been deceitful with him in the first place?

"How about it?" His dark eyes met hers.

She tried to swallow but couldn't. "That would be nice, but I still have to finish some applications. Could you come here to pick me up?"

Clayton studied her. "You'll need some warmer clothes."

"Yes, I know. I'll change and come back. Is that all right?"

"Sure, if that's what you want. I'll pick you up at half past four."

Sophia nodded, her stomach suddenly feeling giddy.

❧

As the winter sun descended into the late afternoon sky, Sophia climbed aboard Clayton's sleigh. Arranging herself comfortably on the seat, she breathed in the frosty air and snuggled into a warm buffalo skin. White-padded tree branches pointed the way as the ground rolled out before the sleigh like a thick carpet of white. The air pricked her cheeks but left no sting behind. The snow fell in soft, fluffy clusters, and Sophia stifled the urge to stick out her tongue and taste the wintry flakes.

The horses settled into a slow, pleasant trot, leaving the city behind them. Sophia felt thankful the fire hadn't reached this far. She looked around her. Sparkling with winter's frost, summer's weeds leaned stiffly against frozen fence posts. Beneath a white coverlet, the harvested fields lay hard as concrete. Meadows once bursting with an array of wildflowers in the summertime now glistened a brilliant white. Sophia shivered slightly. She wasn't sure if she was cold or just trembling with pure delight.

Lightheartedness drifted through her like floating snowflakes on a dusky sky. Imagine, her first sleigh ride! If only she could tell Papá. She wanted to share it with Mammá but felt a little deceitful about not having Clayton meet her yet. Why must she be ashamed of their financial state? God loved everyone the same—she knew that. It shouldn't matter what people thought, and it didn't. . .except for Clayton, of course. Papá always said that as long as a person worked hard at a respectable job to provide the best he could, there was nothing of which to be ashamed.

Clayton turned to her. "You having a good time?" His lips parted, revealing straight, white teeth.

Pure pleasure coursed through her. "Very."

Once they entered the open prairie, Sophia took in the sights. She wanted to remember every single detail. In the distance, a soft breeze lifted a snowy veil, swirling the light mist into tiny sparkling funnels, which quickly dissipated. The beauty of the scene took her breath away.

"Sophia Martone, although we have worked closely together for almost two months, I have much to learn about you," Clayton said as he searched her face for clues.

Her thoughts scrambled. Although she knew she would have to tell him that she wasn't wealthy like he probably assumed, she would not allow anything to spoil their wonderful sleigh ride. Cleverly, she turned the attention back to him. "I have much to learn about you too." She added with a hint of mischief, "How do I know you don't have a sordid past?"

He wiggled his eyebrows and said with a smirk, "Time will tell, dear lady. Time will tell." They shared a laugh. "You are quite a woman."

She could feel heat climbing her face despite the cold and nervously smoothed the buffalo skin over her lap. "I don't know why you would say that."

Sleigh bells jangled softly through the quiet air as the horses' hooves tapped a muffled beat against the snowy trail.

"You work hard helping others, always putting them before yourself, even when you get in trouble."

"What do you mean?" she asked, lifting her chin with a certain amount of defiance.

"I suspect there is a stubborn streak locked inside that pretty head of yours. I've seen Mrs. Adams tell you to go home on several occasions, but you refused her and continued to work late into the evening."

"And Mr. Hill, have you not done the same?"

He coughed. "All right, so we're both stubborn." They laughed together again.

"Tell me about yourself, Sophia. How big is your family? How long have you been in Chicago? What are your dreams?" The questions began to pour from Clayton, making Sophia uncomfortable.

"There's not much to tell, really." She shrugged, wanting desperately to change the subject. She avoided details, giving him a slight sketch.

They came upon a thicket of bushes, and a quick movement caught Sophia's attention. "Look! Something is trapped over there." Seizing the opportunity to talk about something else, she pointed to the struggling object in the tangle of brush.

Clayton pulled to the side of the road. He helped Sophia from the sleigh, and the two of them went to investigate.

Upon their arrival, they found a furry rabbit caught in the underbrush. Sophia gasped. "Poor little thing." Though she read hesitation in Clayton's face, she wasn't about to leave the creature to die there. She just didn't have it in her.

"We must be careful not to get too close to him," Clayton cautioned. "He's scared, and he might scratch."

Holding little concern for herself, Sophia concentrated on freeing the bunny. Clayton reluctantly joined her, and they worked all around the area, pulling away twigs and brush and chipping away at the ice that had formed on the bare outer branches. Finally freed, the little animal shook vigorously and scampered across the open field before they could blink.

"I think you missed your calling, Miss Martone."

Sophia turned a puzzled look his way.

"You should have been a veterinarian," he said with a chuckle. "You were quite determined to free the little guy."

"I can't help myself. There's something about seeing helpless creatures that pulls me to help them."

Clayton escorted her into the sleigh.

"I really should return to the center, Clayton. Mr. Higgins will be there shortly to take me home."

"Are you certain I can't take you home?"

"Quite certain. I have a few things to pick up at the Relief Center." Seeing his disappointment, she quickly added, "Thank you for offering."

He smiled. "All right, but you know I would be happy to wait."

"Thank you, but Mr. Higgins will already be on his way."

Clayton nodded understanding. He gave the reins a snappy jerk and set the sleigh into motion.

They rode the rest of the way back, talking about their

work at the Relief Center and trivial matters. Before Sophia knew it, the magical sleigh ride slipped into the pages of her memories.

❧

Dusk had fallen upon the city as Clayton made his way home. His thoughts drifted to Sophia's determination to free the rabbit. The vision of her rosy cheeks and vibrant brown eyes sent a shiver through him. Her delicate hands had worked quickly to rescue the little creature. Clayton thought of Sophia's work with the people at the Relief Center. No doubt about it, she was a nurturing person. She reminded him of someone, but whom? Someone caring. . .was it the young woman in the journal? Of course. Maybe that's what drew him to both of them—their compassionate natures. Who knew for sure? One thing he did know, he would like to get to know them both better.

Clayton shifted against the chill of the night air. Lantern light flickered from neighboring homes, and he allowed himself to think no more. He listened to the quiet *clip-clop* of the horses' hooves, and contentment settled over him. It had been a good day, and he was glad he had shared it with Sophia.

❧

"What a charming little shop," Alice Nottinger exclaimed as she walked through the entrance, running a gloved hand over the top of a chair.

"Oh, yes," Catherine Forrest agreed, her voice reflecting sincerity. She untied her hat and pulled it off, absently tucking stray hairs into place.

"Thank you," Sophia replied sincerely. "Feel free to look around while I go in the back to get your dresses." Sophia left the room while the two women browsed through the shop.

When she returned, excited words filled the shop as Mrs. Nottinger and Mrs. Forrest examined the gowns Sophia brought out for their inspection. The dresses were nearly completed the week before, but after her shop opened, she brought them in and put the finishing touches in place.

"Miss Martone, they are so exquisite!" Alice Nottinger exclaimed.

"Quite!" Catherine Forrest added.

Sophia breathed a sigh of relief.

"My daughter will love this!" Mrs. Nottinger said as she examined the pink silk evening dress. "This is just like the one I saw in *Godey's Lady's Book,* Sophia." The woman was almost breathless with excitement.

Sophia smiled, remembering the picture she had seen of a similar dress in that book. The lower skirt was trimmed with puffs of white silk, divided by bands of pink silk lace and small bows. The overskirt was open in the back with intricate lace parading around the edges.

"I can't believe the detail," Mrs. Nottinger muttered, running her fingers along the tiny stitching. She turned to Catherine. "Sophia did all this without a single fitting! Mary's been busy with her social affairs and unable to get over here. Sophia took the measurements I gave her and came up with this."

Mrs. Forrest looked on with wide-eyed wonder.

"Mary will certainly mesmerize Clayton Hill when she dons this enchanting dress. At least, if I could ever get him over to see it!"

Sophia's head jerked up at the mention of Clayton's name, then quickly turned away to hide her surprise.

Mrs. Forrest chuckled. "Alice Nottinger, don't tell me you're trying to trap that poor young man for your daughter!"

A conspiring smirk lifted the corners of Alice Nottinger's mouth, as she ran her hands across the folds of the dress. "After all, he is the most eligible bachelor in town." She raised her chin, turning up her nose a bit. "Besides, Mary is just the type of woman he needs—one of social standing and grace."

"Alice, you're positively ruthless." Mrs. Forrest turned her attention back to her dress. Her order had been for a purple velveteen walking suit with two skirts, the lower one just touching the ground, edged with a quilling of black satin. Sophia held her breath, hoping Mrs. Forrest liked it. After thoroughly examining the garment, she exclaimed, "Lovely job, Miss Martone. We will send our drivers back this afternoon with the money."

"Thank you," Sophia said, walking them to the door.

Mrs. Forrest turned before leaving. "I have friends in need of a dressmaker, and I shall highly recommend you."

Mrs. Nottinger nodded her agreement.

"Thank you, again." Sophia waved good-bye and closed the door behind them.

The pleasure she had from the two ladies' approval was overshadowed by her deceit. Mrs. Nottinger's words haunted her. *Mary is just the type of woman he needs—one of social standing and grace.* "If Clayton knew I was poor, he would not care for me," she muttered to herself. Tears filled her eyes. "I've been living a dream."

"It's good to dream, Sophia," her father had told her.

"Yes, to dream, Papá, but not to lie!" she said as she lifted her skirts and escaped to the back room of her shop before anyone could witness her tears.

❧

Clayton bent over to kiss his mother. "Sorry you still have that cough, Mom. Hope you get to feeling better," he said as he turned to go. "See you tonight."

"Oh, Clayton?"

He turned back around.

"I promised Mrs. Baird I'd get this book I borrowed back to her today." She held the book up for him to see. "Do you think you could drop it by her house for me?" she asked, before surrendering to another coughing spell.

"Be happy to, Mom." He walked over and took it from her hands. "I'll drop it by after I leave the Relief Center."

His mother waved an embroidered handkerchief at him,

while she continued coughing. Clayton slipped through the front door.

⁂

Clayton's mind was on Sophia as he drove the carriage home for the noon meal. He still didn't know where she lived. Every time he asked to take her home, she had an excuse.

It seemed, too, each time he tried to find out more about her, she found a way to change the subject. He was beginning to feel like she didn't want him to know anything about her.

His heart wavered between Sophia and the writer of the journal. They both possessed a certain charm, and each stood strong in difficult times. Sophia was here, but she kept him at a distance, making him always wonder what was inside of her. The writer revealed her heart, yet he might never find her.

Before he had time to think further, he noticed the bound copy of *Little Women* on the seat beside him. He glanced around at the homes on Park Lane until he spotted Mrs. Baird's residence. He slowly pulled the horses over. Grabbing the book, he carried it to the front door.

"Clayton Hill, how nice to see you," Mrs. Baird exclaimed. "Please, do come in."

Clayton stepped into the entrance, closing the door behind him.

"Come join me in the sitting room, won't you?"

Clayton had a lot to do at the center and didn't have time for a visit, but he didn't want to hurt her feelings. Mrs. Adams wouldn't mind if he came back a little later than usual. He followed Mrs. Baird. "Mom wanted me to return this," he said, handing her the book.

"Oh, thank you. I know she's been feeling poorly. She didn't have to worry about returning it today."

"Agnes, I—" The woman who entered stopped abruptly when she saw him sitting on the settee. "Oh, I apologize, I didn't realize you had a visitor."

"Not at all, Angelica. Come in here, please."

Clayton stood politely as Mrs. Baird proceeded with the necessary introductions. "Martone?" he repeated, eyebrows arched. "Are you related to Sophia Martone?"

Her eyes twinkled. "She is my daughter. Do you know her?"

"Yes, I do. I work with her at the Relief Center. She is a very nice young lady."

Mrs. Martone glanced at Mrs. Baird, whose mouth stretched into a wide grin as she winked. "Come on, the two of you need to sit down," Mrs. Baird urged.

"I've never seen you before. Do you live nearby?"

Mrs. Martone tipped her head slightly. "It's quite a long story, but yes, as a matter of fact, we live here. The fire drove us to this place."

Mrs. Baird added quickly, "And I'm very glad it did!" With some effort, she rose from her chair. "I'm going to get some tea, and I'll be right back."

Clayton couldn't leave now. Finally, he could learn something about his mysterious Sophia.

"Our home burned in the fire, and Agnes has been gracious enough to allow us to stay here with her." Mrs. Martone's expression reflected her appreciation. "And where is your home?"

Clayton relaxed against the settee. "About two blocks down the road."

They continued in light conversation. Soon Mrs. Baird returned to the room. She carefully poured hot tea into china cups and placed them before them.

"Thank you," Sophia's mother said, raising the cup to her lips.

"I'm sorry about your house. It's been difficult for many people," he said sincerely. "It seems like our work at the Relief Center is never done." He reached over and lifted his cup.

"Sophia works late many days. Between the Relief Center and her shop, she's exhausted most of the time," Mrs. Martone said thoughtfully.

"She has a shop?" He tilted his head, puzzled.

Mrs. Baird jumped in. "Oh, yes, her place is called 'The Thread Bearer.' Have you seen it?"

Clayton rubbed his jaw as he pondered this new information. "Yes, as a matter of fact, I did notice the shop the other day. Mother made a comment about checking it out."

Mrs. Baird jumped in enthusiastically. "I knew it. Our girl is going to have more business than she could imagine! She is quite talented, you know."

"Yes," Clayton agreed. He wondered why Sophia had never mentioned anything about her shop or living with Mrs. Baird. He found the news puzzling.

Mrs. Baird asked how things were going at the Relief Center, and Clayton spent the remainder of his time filling them in on the progress.

Clayton finally drained his teacup and glanced at his pocket watch. "Oh, I apologize, but I must be going."

"Of course. So glad you could visit with us," Mrs. Baird said, escorting him to the front door.

Before leaving, he turned to the two women. "Would you mind not telling Sophia I came over? I'd like to surprise her and drop by for a visit tonight, with your permission, Mrs. Martone?"

Mrs. Martone smiled warmly. "Certainly."

He waved good-bye, then headed down the road, wondering again why Sophia hadn't told him these things.

twelve

"The meal was wonderful, Mammá, as always," Sophia said as she sat comfortably in her usual spot in front of the fireplace.

Mrs. Baird settled into her rocker in the sitting room for their nightly tea and agreed, "Yes, quite, Angelica."

Mammá stuffed another chunk of wood into the blazing fire, brushed her hands together to remove any wooden debris, then sat down.

The hearth blazed with warmth, and the trio slipped into a comfortable silence.

Sophia placed her teacup on the stand beside her and picked up the book. "Oh, *Little Women* is one of my favorite books," she exclaimed, lightly flipping through the pages. She paused and glanced up. "I didn't know you had a copy."

Mrs. Baird feigned a cough. Mammá shifted nervously in her seat.

"Yes, I bought it some time ago," Mrs. Baird said after regaining her composure.

Sophia put the book aside.

"Did you know the author was a nurse in the Civil War?" Mammá interrupted before Sophia could ask any more questions about the book.

Sophia shook her head.

"It's true. What a remarkable lady."

A lengthy pause followed.

"Mrs. Baird, what happened to your husband?" Sophia asked, then quickly inserted, "If you would rather not talk about it, I certainly understand."

Mrs. Baird placed her teacup on its saucer. "Oh, no, Dear, it's quite all right." Her eyes seemed to blur, her gaze held fast to the burning logs snapping in the fireplace. Sophia and her mother waited patiently for the words that would come.

"Henry was killed in the Civil War. A member of the 37th Illinois Battalion. He believed in the Cause. Believed everyone should have a chance at freedom, no matter what his skin color. I didn't want Henry to go, but I knew I could never ask him to compromise his beliefs."

A solemn mood swept across the room. Twigs snapped and crackled from the hearth. Sophia wished she hadn't brought up the subject. Her mother's face held sympathy. Sophia wondered if her mother was remembering the loss of her own husband.

"The enemy didn't get him, though. Sickness did. Pneumonia. They didn't have proper food or clothing." Mrs. Baird continued to stare into the fireplace, as if seeing the events of an earlier time play out in the burning logs. She finally turned sorrowful eyes toward Sophia. "Henry wasn't one to give up." The older woman brushed away a solitary tear that clung to the tip of her eyelashes. "I miss him, but I know his principles and his faith in Jesus Christ gave him the courage to meet death."

Sophia got up from her chair and knelt in front of Mrs. Baird. Her hands were lying quietly on her lap. Sophia grabbed the velvety, wrinkled hand of her friend and held it firmly. "I'm sorry. He must have been a wonderful man to have you for his wife."

Mrs. Baird's eyes brightened. She patted Sophia's arm. "I am the lucky one, Dear. He left me worldly riches, but much more than that, he taught me true wealth comes from investing in the lives of people." Mrs. Baird looked straight into Sophia's eyes and said tenderly, "That's why I do the things I do." Looking back into the fire, she whispered, "Yes, I'm the lucky one."

A knock interrupted their conversation. "I'll get it." Sophia felt like when she'd been doused with cold water when she opened the door. She choked back a gasp.

Amusement flickered in Clayton's eyes when they met hers. No hiding now. He knew where she lived. Sophia figured he wouldn't be taking her on any more carriage rides. Her heart sank at the thought. She cared for him more than she wanted to admit. *Oh, why did he have to come here?*

A gust of wind whipped past Clayton, nearly blowing off his hat. He held it firmly in place. "Um, may I come in?"

The sudden burst of wintry chill brought Sophia to her senses. "Oh, yes. I'm sorry. Do come in."

She led the way into the sitting room, then took his woolen black coat and hat. "Hello, Clayton," Mrs. Baird said.

Sophia turned to make the necessary introductions. "Mammá, this is Clayton Hill. Clayton, my mother, Angelica Martone."

"Hello, Ma'am," he said with a wink and a nod.

"And I believe you know Mrs. Baird?"

"Yes, good to see you again, Ma'am."

"I hope you two don't mind, but we have chores in the kitchen to attend, so if you'll excuse us, please," Mammá said, smiling at Clayton.

Sophia's stomach knotted. She knew he would confront her with her deceit. How she longed to crawl in a hole and cover the opening from perceptive eyes.

Clayton stopped at the stone hearth and rubbed his hands in front of the warm fire. The smell of sweetened tea mingled with the scent of burning pine, filling the room with a pleasant aroma.

"Would you like some tea or coffee?"

"Thank you, no." He sat down on the settee. Sophia eased into Mrs. Baird's rocker across from him.

"I just thought I'd stop by for a few minutes."

"Oh," she said, avoiding his eyes. She fidgeted nervously with her hands. "How did you know I lived here?" she asked, finally breaking the silence.

Clayton explained about the book and his visit earlier in the day.

"I see." More silence. "Are you sure I can't get you something to drink?" she asked politely. She couldn't think of anything to talk about.

"No, thank you. I can't stay long."

Sophia cringed inside. She couldn't remember when she had felt so uncomfortable.

Clayton ran his finger along the collar of his shirt for the fifth time.

It does seem rather warm, Sophia thought. She could feel the heat in her cheeks. Her heart thumped so hard, she was sure Clayton would hear if not for the popping logs.

Conversation was sporadic. Lulls came and went, with more pause than conversation. Sophia felt Clayton's gaze on her but couldn't bring herself to look at him. She shifted uneasily on the rocker, running her hands along her brown skirt to smooth out imaginary wrinkles.

"Have I done something wrong?" he asked, his eyes earnestly seeking for answers.

"No, not at all," she tried to assure him, yet all the while wondering exactly what his motive was for coming to their home. Did he come to make fun of her? To ask her why she had deceived him? To show her he knew she was a poor girl living with a rich friend? Anger slowly began to surge through her, then picked up momentum with every beat of her heart.

"You seem different tonight." He looked at her intently, as if staring would help him read her thoughts.

She searched for the words to get her out of this uncomfortable situation. "Oh, it's just—I—I have a headache," she blurted out too quickly.

"I see," Clayton said. "It's time for me to leave anyway." He stood to get his wraps. Sophia got up from her chair. "I hope you start feeling better," he said as he pulled on his coat and hat.

"Thank you, Clayton." Her words were short and crisp.

They walked silently to the door. He turned to her. "Good night, Sophia."

They stared at one another for a long moment before she found her voice. "Good night."

Clayton adjusted his hat, then turned and walked out the door into the snowy evening.

❧

In her bedroom, Sophia fumed. *Why did he come over?* Did he come over to gloat? To make her feel inferior? Stubbornness swept through her like a spring storm. "So let him. I don' care! He belongs with snobs like Mary Nottinger!"

Sophia looked at her image in the looking glass and spoke sharply. "Sophia Martone, you know he's not at all like that You're forgetting all the qualities you love about him!" She pulled her hand to her mouth and stared in surprise. "I said 'love'!" She walked around her room. "Do I love Clayton Hill?"

She hadn't thought about it until this very moment, but her heart beat out a resounding *Yes!*

thirteen

Clayton found solace from the pages of the journal. Sophia's behavior had wounded him. Her cold treatment made no sense. Maybe he misunderstood her friendship. Did she think him too forward for going to her home? Perhaps she had been expecting another gentleman caller?

He straightened his shoulders. It didn't matter, anyhow. Until now, he had gotten along fine without a woman in his life; he could do it again.

The crisp pages crackled as he opened the journal.

January 15, 1867. Papá used to talk about a verse in the Bible that said if we trust in the Lord with all our hearts and not in our own understanding, if we acknowledge Him, He will direct our paths. I found the verse in his Bible today! It's Proverbs 3:5–6. Papá had the verse written on a piece of paper, and he wrote these words beside it: "We have moved to America!"

I feel so happy when I read his thoughts on the Bible. Papá believed God brought us to America. Since I believe my papá walked with God, I believe, too, God brought us here. If He brought us here, then He will not leave us. He will help us, like Mammá says, even if Papá is not here. I think I like that verse too, Papá!

Every week, my pain feels a little lighter.

Clayton closed the journal and pulled out the Bible in his stand. He read his Bible at church when the pastor referred to the Scriptures in a sermon, but he never made a point of reading it any other time. He wasn't even sure where to begin. Flipping through the pages, it all seemed unfamiliar. He felt like he was stuck in a room with a casual acquaintance and had to listen to conversation on a subject about which he knew nothing.

Why did he feel awkward? It wasn't like he was a heathen exactly. After all, he did go to church. Yet, something inside him told him there had to be more to this than just attending church.

Sophia and the journal writer both talked about the Bible as if it were an old friend. As Clayton stared at the Bible in his hands, he wanted to see the richness of it, to discover in it the treasure they had.

He blew most of the dust from the cover, then wiped his arm across the leather to remove what was left. The pages stirred quietly as he opened it to Proverbs and read through chapter three, verses five and six. "Trust in the Lord with all thine heart; and lean not unto thine own understanding. In all thy ways acknowledge him, and he shall direct thy paths." Clayton pondered the words.

The idea of having a personal relationship with God overwhelmed Clayton. He paused to mull things over. He wondered how God could care about one man's insignificant life. Over the next few hours, he traveled through the pages of the Bible. The words told him God did, indeed, care about his life and wanted a personal relationship with him.

His emotions alternated back and forth between guilt for his sin and awe at God's mercy for sinners. He searched through the pages until his eyes stung.

Finally closing the book, he stared ahead but saw only the uncleanness of his soul. He had not trusted in the Lord with all his heart but rather trusted in himself, his job, his money. He didn't have a personal relationship with God. He only heard stories and sermons about the Creator. While the pastor talked personally with God, Clayton merely eavesdropped. Now he realized not only pastors could have that type of conversation with God, but he could too.

Could he learn to trust God with his future? What future? Would it hold the faceless writer of the journal, Sophia, or someone else? Maybe he would live life alone. Confusion filled him. He was tired of traveling aimlessly through life with no direction, no faith.

He covered his face with his hands. Deep emotion filled every word. "I want to know You, Jehovah God. You're real in the journal writer's life. It's plain to see You in Sophia's life. Will You be real in my life, Lord? I want to walk with You as this woman's father did, trust You for every need, surrender every fear to You, every joy. Forgive me of my complacency and ingratitude. You provide for me daily, and I don't even bother to say thanks. I haven't included You in my life, but I want to change. All I am is Yours. Take control of me from this point forward, Lord."

Clayton rarely cried, but on this occasion, heavy sobs and hushed whispers of surrender alternated back and forth like the ebb and flow of an ocean tide. Finally, wrapped in deep humility, he worshipped the One who had changed his heart. Breathing deeply, he felt confident he had connected with the God of the Universe.

❧

The smell of bacon sizzling in the cast-iron skillet, biscuits baking, and hot coffee lured Clayton into the kitchen. The sun's rays peered through beige lace curtains, bathing the room with light.

His mother appeared to be feeling much better now, humming happily as she fussed over breakfast preparations. Clayton looked after her. He marveled that though they had the financial means for help around the house, his mother insisted on doing things herself. She cared little about impressing people but rather prided herself in handling the affairs of her own household.

"Good morning," she said, casting a sideways glance, then

turned her attention back to the crackling bacon.

"Morning." He began to tell her of his prayer the night before and his new faith.

His mother stopped her preparations and slid into the seat beside him, tears swimming in her eyes. She wiped her face with the hem of her apron. "Clayton, how wonderful." She grabbed his hand and squeezed it.

His father entered just then. "Am I missing something?"

The two looked up at him, their faces wet with tears. Clayton shared his story as his mother collected their breakfast.

Now his father got misty-eyed. "Mary Amanda, our prayers have been answered!"

She nodded and brushed back the fresh tears.

"Your mother and I have been praying for you, Clayton. I know God will guide you." He patted his son's arm.

Over breakfast, they discussed their spiritual journey. Clayton learned his parents had been praying a long time for him to find God in a personal way. Memories played in his mind, and for the first time, he could see how important God was to his mom and dad. Although his folks were somewhat quiet people, he could see God was just as real in their lives.

After the excited talk, the room grew quiet as they worked their way through breakfast.

"I've decided to place an ad for the trunk in the *Chicago Tribune*," Clayton announced before he bit into a crunchy piece of bacon.

His mother straightened the linen napkin on her lap. "Good idea." She glanced at her husband. "Thomas, I don't know why we hadn't thought of it before!"

He shrugged and scooped a mouthful of scrambled eggs onto his fork.

His mother took a drink of milk. "Are you going to the newspaper office today, Clayton?"

He nodded.

"Remember they've moved, so you'd better check the paper

for their new location," his father chimed in before munching on a bite of toast with strawberry jam.

"Yeah, I remember."

Spreading some more jam across his toast, his father added, "Let's pray they read the paper." He quickly shoved the last bite into his mouth.

❧

"Why, Clayton Hill, someone told me I would find you here." The shrill voice caused Sophia to look up and see a young woman dressed in deep purple ruffles and lace standing across from Clayton. Though the Relief Center was housed in a church, a dismal brown loomed in the place. With all the work to be done, little thought was given to decorating. Only now did Sophia become aware of its drab interior. She glanced around the room. Even the workers were dressed in plain, earthy tones. Very little color could be found anywhere.

The woman looked out of place in all her finery against the stark dreariness of the Relief Center. Anyone could easily see she was a woman of social graces. She lifted her delicate, gloved hand to Clayton.

"Mary Nottinger, how are you?" He clasped her hand in a friendly manner.

Sophia's stomach tightened, her breaths became shallow. *So this is Mary Nottinger.*

Sophia got up and busied herself behind a filing cabinet, peeking nonchalantly around the corner at the couple. She knew she should be ashamed for eavesdropping, but she couldn't help herself.

"I've missed you, Clayton. Why haven't you come to see me?" Mary's face crinkled, her voice raised to a slight whine.

Clayton coughed and looked around. Sophia ducked her head back behind the cabinet. When he started talking, she peeked back at them once again.

"I've been busy, Mary, as you can see." He pointed toward the stacks of paperwork on his desk.

Mary's gaze quickly brushed across his desk with disinterest. She shifted with uneasiness and began to swing the hook of the parasol slightly from her hand.

"What brings you here?" Clayton's deep voice caused a stirring inside of Sophia.

"You, of course."

Sophia bristled at the woman's bold response. Someone walked past. To appear busy, Sophia pulled a file from the cabinet, leafed through it, and tucked it back into place. She scraped her finger on the edge of the cabinet, adding to her irritations.

"I had heard you were working here and decided to rescue you from this place and invite you to our home for supper this Saturday." Mary batted her eyelashes. Sophia gaped as she watched the young lady spinning her web, like a spider trapping its poor victim.

"That's very kind of you, but—"

"Now I won't take no for an answer, Clayton Hill," she interrupted, her lower lip protruding into a childlike pout.

Clayton conceded. "All right, I'll be there."

Sophia flinched.

Mary smiled with satisfaction. "Wonderful! How about seven o'clock?"

"I'll see you then," he replied.

Sophia bit her lip and watched as Mary's eyes bore into Clayton's, neither of them blinking. Sophia felt as if her own heart stopped beating.

"I'll be waiting," Mary said in a voice dripping with charm.

She turned to leave, and men all over the room cleared the way as she dramatically made her exit. Sophia watched as every male stood, dreamily following Mary with his gaze.

Clayton sat down and got back to work.

Sophia clamped her gaping mouth shut when Mary finally went through the doors. Looking back at Clayton, Sophia slammed the drawer of the filing cabinet harder than she intended. Clayton looked up with a start. She quickly turned away and stomped out of the room.

~

"No matter how long I live, I'll never understand women," Clayton said, resting his hand against the wooden mantel. He stared into the stone hearth that divided a full wall lined with volumes of books. The room smelled of leather binding and burning logs.

His father put down his paper. "You want to talk about it?" he asked, giving his full attention to his son.

Clayton exhaled deeply, making his way toward a chair across from his father.

His mother briefly interrupted their conversation, offering coffee, but he refused. He couldn't eat or drink anything right now. She must have recognized they were having a man-to-man talk; she quickly turned on her heels and made a hasty retreat.

Clayton sat for a moment, trying to think of how to explain his dilemma. He stared blankly at the thick rug stretched before him. After a few moments, he looked up at his dad, who waited patiently. "Dad, I've told you about Sophia Martone from the Relief Center?"

"Yes, you've mentioned her. I believe you were going to ask her to dinner before you got sick?"

Clayton nodded.

Before Clayton could respond further, his father continued. "She lives with Agnes Baird, right?"

"Yes, she's the one."

"What about her?"

"It seems I've upset her somehow, and I don't know what I've done. We were getting along fine, then things seemed to change. Now, she's very professional in her manner toward me." Clayton's gaze turned toward the dancing blue flames in the hearth.

"I take it she's special to you?" his father probed.

"Yes, she is." He pulled his gaze from the flames and turned back to his dad.

"I see." His father seemed to ponder the situation. "When did you notice the change?"

"That's just it, I'm not sure. Seems like it was around the time I visited her at Mrs. Baird's house. I surprised her, and maybe she doesn't like to be surprised." He took a deep breath and let out a sigh. "Oh, I don't know." His words were tight, lined with exasperation.

"What about Mary Nottinger? Your mother tells me you're going there Saturday for supper."

Clayton waved his hand. "Oh, we're just friends. I don't even want to go, but it seemed the polite thing to do."

"Does Mary know you're just friends?"

Clayton's distant gaze refocused on his father. "What?"

"Does Mary know you're just friends?"

"Certainly, I would assume so. We've been friends since we were children."

"Are you sure she doesn't think it something more?" his father pressed.

Clayton thought for a moment. "She did seem rather strange when she came into the center." He remembered the scene.

"And was Sophia around?"

"Uh, no, I don't remember Sophia." His words stopped short. He suddenly remembered the loud noise of the closing filing cabinet and Sophia's sharp glance his way before leaving the room in a hurry. "Wait. I think I do remember her being in there."

"Ah." His father nodded his head in a knowing manner, suggesting he knew more than he was telling.

"What?" Clayton asked, confused.

His father shrugged. "My son, the ways of women are difficult, if not impossible, to understand at times." He paused a moment, allowing Clayton time to think on the situation.

The situation perplexed him. With frustration, he combed

s fingers through his hair.

"But if I were you, I'd be very careful. You don't want to rt either young lady."

Clayton considered his father's words.

Walking over, his father placed his hand on Clayton's oulder. "I'll be praying for you, Son." With light steps, he rned and walked out of the library, leaving Clayton alone ith his churning thoughts.

fourteen

Mary Nottinger stood perfectly still in The Thread Bearer
Sophia stuck the last pin in place, marking the final seam.

"There, that should do it." Sophia wrote the measuremen
on a slip of paper.

Mary shrugged out of the heavy material, down to h
bustle and petticoat. Sophia helped her slip back into h
original dress.

Sophia drew back the curtains and stepped out of th
dressing area with Mary following closely behind.

Scanning her notes, Sophia said, "I don't believe I'll ha
any trouble altering this dress for you, Miss Nottinger."

"Good. But do call me Mary. Now—Sylvia, is it?"

Before Sophia had time to respond, Mary continued. "Yo
must have this dress ready and delivered to my home t
Friday night. I have an important engagement on Saturda
and I want to look perfect."

"I understand." Her voice chilled, knowing the engage
ment was with Clayton.

Mary walked in front of the looking glass and began t
poke at her hair, tucking loose strands, looking quite please
with her own reflection. "By the way, you do a nice job," sł
said, her eyes never leaving her reflection.

"Thank you," Sophia replied, carefully folding the thic
layers of cloth.

Mary's voice droned on of society parties and her superf
cial life. If she noticed Sophia's half-interest in the convers
tion, Mary didn't show it.

"Is this all you do, Sylvia—just dressmaking?" she aske
incredulously, as if Sophia must live the dreariest of lives.

"It's Sophia, and no, I also work at the Relief Center," Sophia said, as she pushed the last fold of blue material into a box with more force than necessary.

Mary turned away from her reflection and narrowed her eyes. "Oh, then you must know Clayton Hill."

"Yes, I do," Sophia acknowledged, busying herself, picking up tiny pins. Feeling the scrutiny of Mary's penetrating eyes, Sophia continued to tidy up the area.

Mary lifted her chin as she ran her hands across her dress, smoothing the ruffles. "Funny, he never mentioned you. But then, why would he?" Snootiness edged her voice. "I must tell him you're my *dressmaker.*"

Sophia's head jerked up; her eyes met Mary's gaze. Mary smiled haughtily.

Sophia blinked and attempted to swallow her rising anger. "I'm closing the shop early on Friday, but I'll deliver your dress to you by five o'clock," she managed through the lump in her throat.

Mary stared at her for a moment, then reached for her parasol. "Fine," she said, as if dismissing the matter entirely.

Sophia thought if Mary lifted her chin any higher, she'd fall backwards for sure. Her stroll toward the door took on the very air of snobbery. They said their polite good-byes. Sophia watched as Mary stepped through the door, opened her parasol, and gave it a dainty swirl before glancing back at the door with a smirk. Sophia forced a smile and prayed a quick prayer of forgiveness for wanting to kick Mary right in the bustle.

❧

It was midday when Mr. Higgins pulled the carriage to a stop in front of the Nottingers' homestead. The stately brick dwelling sprawled across a neatly trimmed lawn sprinkled with the day's newly fallen snow. Sophia climbed out of the carriage with the box holding Mary's dress, the dress she would be wearing during her supper with Clayton tomorrow night. Feeling a fresh wave of pain, Sophia chased the thought away. She walked on to the porch and tapped her knuckles against the wooden door.

A well-dressed, older man answered. "Yes, Ma'am?"

"I am Sophia Martone, and I have a package for Mary Nottinger."

Sophia heard Mary squeal in the background. Just then, Mary pushed past the butler to the front door. "Do come in, Sylvia," she said excitedly.

"Sophia," she corrected, wondering if Mary had a memory problem or just wanted to make her feel insignificant.

"Oh, yes. Sophia." Mary snatched the box from Sophia's hands and began tearing it open.

Sophia stepped into their expansive hallway. She tried not to gape at the crystal chandelier sparkling overhead. Caught in the afternoon sunbeams, each prism cast a rainbow across the marble flooring.

Mary pulled the garment from the box and carefully examined the alterations.

Mrs. Nottinger entered the hallway. "Sophia, so good to see you." The half-smile never reached her eyes. In fact, her attention barely focused on Sophia but rather quickly turned toward Mary.

"Mother, what do you think?" Mary showed her mother the alterations.

Mrs. Nottinger tipped her chin. "It looks fine, Dear, providing it will fit." She laughed mockingly, then turned toward Sophia. "But then, I'm sure it will since Sophia altered it for you." Her words dripped with feigned politeness.

Sophia's gaze lowered. "Thank you, Ma'am."

Mary pulled one sleeve out to her arm and began to take large steps across the floor, dancing a waltz in the silent room.

Sophia could understand why this was Mary's favorite dress. The sea blue would bring out her eyes. Her blond hair would make a striking contrast. She would look stunning in the gown. Would Clayton be dazzled by her appearance?

Sophia tried not to frown. No doubt, Mary would look as delicious as a turkey dressed for the Thanksgiving table. *Too bad someone couldn't pluck her feathers,* Sophia thought shamelessly.

"Sophia, did you hear me?" Mrs. Nottinger's words loosened Sophia from anger's grip.

Sophia looked at her with a start. "I'm sorry. Ma'am?"

"I was saying," Mrs. Nottinger repeated impatiently, "I wondered how we got along without you."

Shame began to fringe the edges of Sophia's heart for her hateful thoughts. "Thank you, Ma'am." She fingered her bonnet. "I really must be going now."

Mrs. Nottinger pulled money from her purse and handed it to Sophia. "You've started on our dresses for the Christmas ball?"

"Yes, Ma'am."

"Good. With Thanksgiving just around the corner, Christmas will be fast upon us. I do hope you'll have them ready in time."

"Yes, Ma'am, they will be ready."

"Good. Just let us know when you need our fittings."

Sophia nodded. She glanced at the money Mrs. Nottinger handed her. Sophia's eyes widened in surprise. She turned to Mrs. Nottinger. "Thank you, again."

They waved good-bye, and Sophia made her way to the carriage.

❧

Sophia walked into the kitchen, where her mother stirred a deep pot of soup over the cast-iron stove. "Hello, Mammá," Sophia said as she bent over slightly to kiss her mother on the cheek. Just then, she got a whiff of the simmering beef and vegetables. She took a deep breath and closed her eyes and sighed with pleasure. "Oh, it smells wonderful."

Mammá smiled and continued stirring the chunky stew, causing clouds of steam to rise from the deep kettle.

"Sophia, Abigail O'Connor came by tonight. She wants to talk to you about her dress for the Christmas ball."

"Did she say she would come by the shop?" Sophia asked, as she nibbled at a scrap of carrot left on the counter.

"Yes," her mother replied, tapping the metal ladle lightly against the lip of the pot, then replacing the lid. She turned to Sophia. "She'll be there in the morning."

"Good."

Mrs. Baird entered the room and exchanged greetings with Sophia and her mother. Sophia slipped out of the kitchen while Mrs. Baird and her mother carried on a friendly conversation about the women's suffrage movement.

She went toward her room, thinking of Abigail. Sophia and the twenty-five-year-old redhead had become fast friends. When the O'Connors began attending her church late last spring, Abigail found out about Sophia's sewing talents and employed her to fashion some dresses. They shopped together for dress goods, each trip revealing more and more of their compatibility to one another.

Sophia entered her room and flopped on the bed. Sinking into the soft mattress, she took a deep breath and stared unseeingly at the ceiling.

The O'Connors, though a wealthy family, were nothing like the Nottingers. The O'Connor family generously shared their wealth with those less fortunate. Abigail's family treated everyone the same, regardless of their financial status.

"Thank You, Lord, for my friend," Sophia whispered into the peaceful room. She looked forward to meeting with Abigail in the morning.

Her stomach growled, reminding her of the vegetable soup waiting downstairs. She sprang up at once and prepared herself for dinner.

❧

The bell gave a soft jangle. A rush of cold air swished into the room as Abigail quickly closed the door behind her.

"Good morning, Sophia."

Sophia looked up from her sewing machine and smiled broadly. "Hello, Abby." She stood and walked over to her friend, giving her a quick hug.

Abigail pulled off layers of wraps and began to make herself at home. The icy air had left a cherry stain on her plump cheeks, giving them a healthy glow. She ran long fingers through her loose red curls, attempting to straighten them, but they immediately coiled back into place. Her bright blue eyes sparkled with wonder as she gazed around the room. "I love your shop, Sophia. It is absolutely charming."

"Thanks. I feel very blessed." Sophia turned toward the kitchen and called behind her, "Would you like some tea?"

"That would be lovely."

Sophia turned to see Abigail glancing at an arrangement of recent issues of *Godey's Lady's Book* fanned across the round tabletop.

"Bring some of those with you, if you want to look through them."

Abigail reached for a couple of the publications, then followed Sophia to the back room.

Delicate, light blue curtains framed the kitchen window that overlooked an alley. A teakettle perched atop the tiny black stove. A small sink and cabinet crouched in the corner. Sophia grabbed the kettle and filled it with water, then placed it on the stove, allowing it to simmer softly. "I'm glad they're getting the water situation under control."

Abigail agreed. "I heard the Millers had a little fish come through their faucet. Can you imagine?" The two shared a laugh.

They sat down at the scrubbed table where Sophia usually ate her lunches.

Abigail scanned the latest dress fashions, talking excitedly. "I have a wonderful idea for a dress for our Christmas ball." She turned more pages. "Have you picked your dress yet?"

"What?" Sophia looked startled.

At once, Abigail stopped leafing through the pages and lifted an anxious face toward Sophia. "You are coming, aren't you?" She scooted to the edge of her seat, waiting for Sophia's answer.

Open-mouthed, Sophia stared at her. The question caught her off guard. When at last she found her voice, she asked incredulously, "Me, go to a ball?"

"Of course. I couldn't give my very first Christmas ball without my best friend being there," Abigail pleaded.

"I couldn't possibly—" Sophia began.

Abigail held up her hand and shook her head with great vigor. "I absolutely will not allow you to refuse, Sophia. My heart would break into a million pieces if you said no." Abigail tended to be overly dramatic at times, but admittedly, it was one of the attributes Sophia loved about her friend.

Exasperation balled up inside of Sophia. "What would I wear, Abby? I have nothing for a ball."

"I would happily let you borrow one of mine, but you're much too small for my frocks. Mother and I thought perhaps we could purchase the material for you. . . ."

Before Abigail could continue, Sophia was already shaking her head. She never accepted charity.

"Before you say no, please listen to our idea."

Sophia hesitantly looked at her friend.

"We could purchase the material for your dress," she continued slowly, then wisely added, "and you could deduct the cost of your material from the making of my dress." Abigail's fingers twisted one of her curls as she waited for Sophia's response.

Sophia knew it didn't matter to her friend one way or the other if she received a discount on her dress. The O'Connors had plenty of money to spare. She just wanted to make a way for Sophia to attend the ball. *My dear friend, Abby.* Sophia's gaze drifted from Abigail toward the window as if pondering the idea. "I suppose I could consider—"

Giving no time for Sophia to give it further thought, Abigail broke in with a sigh of relief. "Good. It's all settled then."

Before Sophia could object, the bell sounded in the other room. Sophia rose from her chair and walked to the front of the shop. "Jonathan, you didn't need to work yet tonight. The books can wait until next week, if you'd like."

Jonathan Clark stomped his boots hard just before entering. He appeared breathless from the cold. "No, problem, Sophia. I'd rather get the work done." A cough or two escaped him. Immediately, he set to brushing the snow from his shoulders and arms. Finally looking up, he stopped midsentence as his eyes locked with Abigail's, who was standing just behind Sophia.

"Oh, hello," he said, when he finally found his voice.

Sophia stifled a giggle and made the introductions.

"Sophia didn't tell me she had such a lovely friend."

Abigail blushed beneath his stare. Sophia stood amazed. Never had she seen this charming side of Jonathan. Likewise, she noticed Abigail appeared quite smitten.

"If you'll excuse me for a moment, I will get the books for you, Jonathan," said Sophia, though she may as well have saved her breath. Jonathan barely glanced her way. Already he and Abigail had plunged into comfortable conversation.

Sophia smiled to herself and slipped into the back room, pulling out the shop's ledger books. Hearing the conversation in the other room, she decided to pour herself some more tea, giving her friends time to get to know one another. She leafed through the various pictures of dresses, trying to imagine herself at a Christmas ball. She wasn't sure how long she dreamily browsed through the pages before Abigail rushed into the room.

Abby was positively giddy. She whispered between animated breaths, "Mr. Clark has agreed to come to the Christmas ball!"

Sophia looked at her in shocked surprise.

Abigail met Sophia's expression with defense; her voice took on a serious note. "Well, after all, he needs to meet people in town, being a stranger around here and everything." The two laughed simultaneously. Abigail resumed her perky disposition and squeezed Sophia's hands. "He's so handsome! Why haven't you told me about him?" Not waiting for a response, Abigail brushed through her curls, bent down, and whispered, "Do I look all right?"

"You look wonderful." Before Sophia could utter another word, her friend returned to the front of the shop. Sophia finished her tea and finally closed her fashion books. She rinsed her cup, picked up the ledgers, and went in to join Abigail and Jonathan.

"Here you are, Jonathan," Sophia said as she handed him the books.

"If you'll excuse me, Miss O'Connor." He tapped his finger against his forehead, his eyes lingering on Abigail a little longer than necessary.

"Of course." She smiled demurely.

He walked over to the counter and plunked the thick book in front of him with a sigh. Sophia found it amusing he didn't begin the work with his usual enthusiasm.

She turned her gaze to Abigail, who looked absolutely besotted. Sophia hid her smile as she handed Abigail her cloak. Abigail stood transfixed.

"Abby?" Sophia called to her.

"Oh dear." She pulled her hand to her mouth to hide a giggle. Maneuvering into her coat, Abigail looked once more toward Jonathan.

"Mr. Clark, we shall see you Christmas night then, at the ball?"

He walked over to Abigail. "Only if you will allow me the pleasure of escorting you, Miss O'Connor." He lifted her hand to his lips. Abigail and Sophia exchanged wide-eyed glances.

Abigail clamped her mouth shut when he looked up to her eyes. "Of course," she squeaked, when she finally found her voice.

Jonathan bowed slightly, then returned to his work.

Sophia talked to Abigail as they walked to the door, but she had a feeling Abigail heard nothing but the beating of her own heart.

fifteen

Sophia felt she had barely gotten to work on Monday before the day was almost spent. With the upcoming Christmas ball, she found herself busily poring over books in search of a dress for herself, along with stitching her way through endless ruffles and seams for others. Marie Zimmerman handled most of the alterations for Sophia's customers, while Sophia concentrated on making Christmas gowns. She realized she could never have taken all the new business if not for Marie's help.

Once again, she learned to trust God's timing. Seth Zimmerman's health had improved, enabling him to obtain a job and help their family.

Poking her head up from the sewing area, Sophia peeked out the window at the dusky sky. She knew her mother would be preparing dinner and decided to call it a day.

Thoughts of the Christmas ball continued to swirl through her mind as she tidied the clutter around her. She had never been to a ball. Sophia assumed Clayton would probably be there with Mary. Would Sophia need someone to accompany her? She couldn't imagine who would take her or whom she would want to take her.

Chewing on the edge of her lip, Sophia glanced at the fashion magazine beside her machine and decided she'd take one last look for a dress before she closed the shop and went home.

Before she had time to sit back down, the front door bell jangled. She looked up with a start.

Clayton Hill walked through the door. His dark eyes met hers.

"Clay—ton," she stammered. "What a surprise." She got up and walked toward him. They hadn't talked much since the night at Mrs. Baird's house. Sophia had purposely avoided him since Mary Nottinger had staked her claim on him.

"I heard about your shop and wanted to take a look." His eyes seemed to challenge her.

She knew there was another reason for his being here. *Mary probably told him I was her seamstress.* Sophia lifted her chin with a confidence she did not feel.

"You're welcome to look around." She gave a great sweep with her hand.

"Thank you."

She talked nervously, pointing to the various items in the shop. He followed her patiently as she took him on the short tour, and they ended back in the middle of the front room.

"So there, you've seen it." She knew her place must not seem like much to him, but for a working woman, this was a dream come true.

Clayton looked down, studying his gloves. Sophia thought he had something to say but didn't know how to say it.

"Why didn't you tell me?" He faced her now. His words came out soft, serious.

"Tell you what?"

"About where you lived, about your shop? It's like you're trying to hide things from me, and I don't understand why." His eyes searched her own so deeply, she wondered if she should cover her heart for fear he would discover her secret love for him.

She owed him an explanation, and she knew it. "I–I didn't think it mattered." She fumbled for words.

He took a step toward her. Sophia's heart raced. Before she could take a step back, he reached for her hands. "Don't you know how much you matter to me?"

Sophia's knees grew weak. "Clayton, I—" The words lodged in her throat. Her gaze fell to the floor.

"Sophia," he said in a whisper. He stood so close, she could almost feel his breath brush against her face. She looked at him and told herself to stop trembling.

Sparkling dark eyes met hers. She saw something in them. To her relief, it wasn't condescension like she'd seen in Mary's eyes. What was it?

"Have I done something wrong?" His tender words stroked her heart.

"No," she could barely croak. His nearness unnerved her, and yet she yearned for it all at the same time. Reluctantly, she tried to slip her hands from his grasp, but he caressed them gently, firmly.

"If I have hurt you in any way, please forgive me. I care about you, Sophia, and I want to continue our friendship."

Sophia looked away. Could he feel her shaking?

Releasing her hands, he cupped and lifted her chin. "I said I care about you, Sophia."

Their eyes locked. She could feel her cheeks flaming. The room began to swirl. Clayton's gaze lowered to her lips. Her mouth went dry. He bent his head toward her. A soft glow seemed to envelop the room. Her skin began to tingle. She wondered if she was going to faint. Just as Clayton's lips settled softly upon hers like an airy breeze, the bell on the door rattled, startling them both.

Like being jerked from a wonderful dream, Sophia felt a bit dazed. She stood perfectly still as Clayton stepped away from her and turned around.

In a matter of seconds, she snapped to attention. The two of them stood speechless as they came face-to-face with Mary Nottinger.

❧

"I thought I wouldn't make it before you closed," Mary said, shutting the door behind her harder than necessary. "Clayton Hill, whatever are you doing here?" Her voice was stern, like a mother scolding her child.

"I—" His words cut off, as if he didn't owe her an explanation.

Mary's eyes were as hard as rocks. She turned back to

Sophia. "Why, Sophia, your face is positively scarlet." Her words pricked with accusation.

Sophia's hands rushed to her face. Before she could open her mouth to explain, Mary cut her off with a wave of her gloved hand.

"Seems everyone has trouble talking these days." With calculating eyes, Mary seemed to assess the situation as she looked from Sophia to Clayton. Then, as if to dismiss her mental wanderings, she said, "Anyway, here's the dress I told you about which needs mending." Mary plopped the piles of ruffles into Sophia's open arms.

Mary turned to Clayton and purred, "Clayton, would you be a dear and take me home? My driver is waiting for me, but he has endless errands to run for Mother. I fear he'll never get them all done if he has to take me home. I shall be terribly devastated if you refuse."

Clayton looked at Sophia. She turned away from him and walked over to the sewing area, placing Mary's clothing in a stack with Mary's other mending to be done.

Clayton coughed once. "Well, I don't know, I—"

"But of course you can, Clayton. You know you don't want to leave my mother pouting over her errands."

Mary was already pulling him toward the door.

He looked at Sophia once more. His expression seemed to plead for a reason to stay. But Sophia offered none.

He heaved a sigh of resignation. "Certainly."

Mary placed her hand in the crook of his arm, then glanced back at Sophia triumphantly. "I'll be back on Wednesday for my dress."

Sophia walked toward them as they edged closer to the door. Clayton stopped and turned to her. "Were we finished with our discussion, then?"

"Clayton." Mary pulled his attention back to her. "Did you know Sophia was my seamstress?" Her voice was icy, demeaning.

"Sophia?"

"Good-bye, Clayton. Mary." Sophia could barely choke out the words before closing the door.

Tears stung Sophia's eyes. She stood motionless in the shadows while she watched them slip into the dusky evening.

❧

"Morning, Sophia," Clayton said as he placed his cloak and hat on the wooden peg inside the hallway of the Relief Center.

"Hello, Clayton." Her words were brisk. She turned abruptly to leave the room.

Clayton practically ran to catch up with her. He grabbed her arm. "About last night—"

"You don't owe me an explanation," said Sophia evenly, trying to keep calm, willing her tears to stay away.

"Sophia," Mrs. Adams called in a happy voice, "could you come over here, please?"

Sophia looked up at Clayton and yanked her arm free. "If you will excuse me, Mr. Hill?" Her eyes dared him to speak further.

❧

"Do you believe him, Abby?" Sophia paced her bedroom, her words revealing the hurt inside her heart. "I can't believe he had the nerve to try to explain it all away to me this morning!" Abigail listened carefully while Sophia continued to vent.

"It's not like Mary twisted his arm. He didn't have to take her home." She stopped in front of Abigail. "Why does he do that? Why does he do everything she asks?" She turned on her heels before Abigail could respond and continued pacing.

"Sophia, come here." Abigail patted the seat beside her on the bed.

Heaving a deep sigh, Sophia shuffled over to Abigail and sat down.

Abigail faced her and grabbed her hand. "Clayton is a gentleman, Sophia. The Nottingers and the Hills have known each other for years. Clayton and Mary went to school together. I believe it's out of respect for her and to keep peace between the families that he does this."

Sophia took a moment to digest her friend's words. The anger inside her seemed to flee with a sigh. "You might be right," she said in a whisper. Suddenly things turned around, and she began to feel bad for her behavior. "Why am I always the one to feel guilty?" Her question hung in the air for a long moment.

"How do you know what he is feeling when you won't even allow him to explain?"

Abigail's usual wisdom came shining through. Sophia finally smiled sideways at her friend and said, "Hey, whose side are you on anyway?" She tossed a pillow at her.

Abigail giggled. "Always yours, my friend." She gave Sophia a gentle hug. "I just don't want you to let go of a good thing until you've thought this completely through."

"Are you saying Clayton is a good thing?" Sophia teased her now.

"Well, he sure ain't bad, Honey!" she said with a phony accent. They laughed together.

"I'm sorry I started telling you all my problems when you walked in the door. I didn't even give you a chance to say why you had come over." Sophia fluffed a pillow against the bedpost and leaned against it for support.

"I can't go ice skating with you and Jonathan." She paused and passed a cautious glance at Sophia before adding, "But I still want you to go."

"What? Why can't you go? And why would I go with him without you?"

"I'm sorry, Sophia, but Mother insists I accompany her to New York. Father has business, and Mother wants me to shop with her." Abigail propped a pillow behind herself now and leaned against the other bedpost. She pouted. "You know I'd much rather go ice skating with you and Jonathan."

"But he asked you! I was only coming along at your insistence. This is so embarrassing." Sophia leaned her head back against the pillow and stared at the ceiling.

"You've just got to go, Sophia. If you don't, one of Mary's friends will snatch him up while I'm gone. This way, you can keep an eye on him."

Sophia looked over to see her friend staring at her.

"Sophia, he knows how you feel about Clayton," she confessed guardedly.

Sophia gasped. "How would he know?"

"Calm down. It's all right." Abigail reached for Sophia's hand and patted it. "He just mentioned he could tell by the way you two look at each other when he's been to the Relief Center to discuss business with you."

Sophia considered this. She hadn't realized she was so transparent with her feelings.

"I really must be going, Sophia." Abigail stood and pleaded one last time, "Please say you'll go."

Sophia sighed heavily. "Oh, all right. If you're sure he won't get the wrong idea."

Abigail gave Sophia a peck on the cheek. "I'm sure. You are my best friend, Sophia. I'll be back in town on Sunday afternoon. We'll catch up then."

Sophia nodded as she walked Abigail down the staircase to the front door.

Abigail turned to her. "Have fun on Friday, but not too much fun."

Sophia made a face, and Abigail laughed her way through the door.

sixteen

"Oh, my. I'm afraid I'm a bit unsteady in these things, Jonathan. It's been a few years since I've tried to ice skate."

He patted his gloved hands together, trying to keep warm. "Don't worry, Sophia. The technique will come back to you." His words lifted with short puffs of air.

Sophia finished pulling her skates up over her shoes. She knocked her knuckles against the pond once more, making sure it would hold her. She hadn't stopped to consider all the skaters gliding around on the frozen pond. Upon seeing this, she finally mustered enough confidence to venture out onto the ice, deciding it must be as hard as steel. She tried to steady herself and threw Jonathan an apologetic grin when she caught him watching her.

A few shredded clouds floated aimlessly along the sky. Sophia shivered slightly as she took a deep breath of the brisk afternoon air. With a glance at the covering of snow on the ground surrounding them, she decided it was a perfect day for skating. Others obviously agreed with her. Never had she seen the pond so full of people.

"Ready to give it a try?" Jonathan extended his arm to her. She threw him a look of uneasiness, then reluctantly reached for him. Slowly, they made their way onto the middle of the pond. He held her steady, carefully gliding her around the ice, picking up a little speed each time they made a full circle.

They talked of his college days back East. He pumped her with endless questions about Abigail. Sophia knew without a doubt Jonathan was quite taken with her friend. *If only Clayton felt the same way about me.*

"Here we go," he was saying. "Time to try it on your own."

He finally let go of Sophia, allowing her to skate freely by herself. She stifled a light scream and laughed as she wobbled, then quickly attempted to steady herself. He slowed his speed, allowing her to catch up, until they finally settled into a comfortable pace and skated side-by-side. They talked of his move to Chicago and how he liked it. He asked her opinion of his chances with Abigail, and Sophia encouraged him as a good friend.

All at once, a group of young boys raced between Sophia and Jonathan, bumping her slightly. She quivered on her skates, and before Jonathan could reach her, she started falling. As she was about to come crashing into a heap upon the icy floor, strong, steady arms lifted her to safety.

She pulled her hand to her throat and tried to catch her breath. With her head bent, she brushed the front of her skirt. "Jonathan, thank you so much. I would have made a complete fool of myself had you not caught me," she said between shallow breaths.

"Glad to be of help, Sophia."

The familiar voice gave her a start. She jerked her head up and looked into the teasing sparkle of Clayton's eyes.

Before she could respond, Mary Nottinger skated up beside him. "Clayton, do be a good boy and fetch my scarf from the carriage."

"But you're already wearing a scarf." Clayton looked at her with frustration.

"I know," she said as she gently touched his arm, "but I'm so cold, and the other one is much warmer."

"Now, look here, Mary—" Clayton's voice sounded as though he was doing all he could to keep from exploding.

She turned to Sophia as if to dismiss him. "So good to see you, Dear." Her words dripped with insincerity.

Clayton pulled in an exasperated breath, looked at Sophia and shook his head, then skated away.

Although Sophia thought he might lose his temper had he

stayed, she fumed that Clayton always gave in to Mary, family friends or not. Suddenly all of Abigail's wise words fluttered away like a flock of sparrows.

"It's a lovely day, isn't it?"

The words were coated with artificial sweetness, annoying Sophia to no end. "Yes, it is," she finally managed. She decided she must not reduce herself to Mary's level. If she did, no doubt she would be playing into Mary's hands. No, Sophia promised herself she would remain calm.

Mary looked over the crowd. "Are you here with Abigail?" She gave a slight chuckle, making Sophia feel like she couldn't possibly have a male escort.

Forced confidence fringed her words. "Actually, no, I'm here with, uh, well—"

Mary tilted her head and raised her brow, waiting for the answer like someone about to receive a juicy bit of gossip.

"Jonathan Clark, as a matter of fact." A tinge of guilt jabbed Sophia's conscience. He wasn't her escort, after all; but it didn't hurt to make Mary think so, did it? Still, Sophia knew she had to stop telling half-truths.

The tension seemed to leave Mary's face. Her shoulders relaxed and her eyes brightened. "Oh, how wonderful!" She clasped her hands together.

Clayton skated up to Mary and carelessly tossed her the scarf.

He went to Sophia's side. "Are you warm enough, or can I get you anything?"

Mary pretended not to notice.

"No, thank you, Clayton." Sophia couldn't help but wonder if a hidden apology lay in his offer. Their eyes met and lingered for a moment. Her stomach flipped. Oh, why couldn't she stay mad at him?

A sneering comment interrupted them. "Clayton, do you know Jonathan Clark?"

Sophia's heart chased her pulse to her throat.

"Yes, I've talked with him a few times at church. Nice fellow. Why do you ask?"

Sophia watched as the other woman's face beamed with pure pleasure. She looked intently at Sophia, then to Clayton, allowing a dramatic pause to emphasize the moment. She swallowed slowly as if the words she was about to say were delicious little morsels meant to be savored. "Oh, you didn't know? He accompanied Sophia today."

Sophia thought Mary's behavior resembled a tattling child.

The color drained from Clayton's face despite the cold. Sophia stared at the toes of her skates.

Jonathan came up behind her. "Are you all right?" he asked, almost out of breath.

Sophia turned around with a start, "Oh, yes, I was just talking with. . .friends."

"Those kids were playing some silly game, and I couldn't get through for the longest time," he explained. He turned to the others. "Good to see you, Miss Nottinger," he said, smiling.

"Yes, it's *very* good to see you, Jonathan." Her words were laced with victory.

Jonathan turned. "Clayton, good to see you again." He extended his hand.

"Jonathan." Clayton returned the handshake.

Mary started conversation about the weather. She and Jonathan engaged in friendly conversation, their voices fading into the background. Sophia's gaze drifted to Clayton. He was already looking at her. His eyes held so many questions. She wanted to answer him but dared not. Doing so might reveal her heart, and she knew she wasn't right for him. How could she fit in with his social standing, when she had worked hard just to survive?

"Don't you agree, Sophia?" The irritating female voice pulled them apart once again.

"I'm sorry?" Embarrassment filled her face with warmth.

"I said the Christmas ball is going to be such fun, don't you agree?"

Sophia could feel her skin growing pasty white. They would know any minute now Jonathan was to be Abigail's escort, not hers. Oh, why did she get herself into these messes?

"Yes," she responded. She tugged at her hair. "You know, I believe I lost one of Mammá's hairpins. Will you excuse me while I search for it, please?" She turned to Jonathan. "Will you help me find it?"

"Certainly."

With that, she abruptly made her exit. She heard Jonathan mumble, "See you later," and skate just behind her.

"We'll never find it here in this crowd, you know," he said as he approached her side.

The skaters in front of Sophia became liquid blurs as she brushed past them, pretending to scan the floor occasionally for the missing hairpin. She skated toward the bench. Plunking herself onto the wooden seat, she bent over and tugged at the straps of her skates. "I'm sorry, Jonathan, I must go home now." Her tears began to drop, making watery circles on the ice beside her feet.

"Are you all right?" Jonathan asked with genuine concern.

"I just want to go home." She yanked at the straps, frantic to get her skates off and get as far away from Clayton and Mary as possible. She finally pulled them free and headed for the buggy. Jonathan struggled to keep up with her.

Just before boarding, she looked back at the pond. Clayton stared in her direction, with Mary tugging at his arm.

Sophia turned away and closed her eyes tight to chase away her mounting emotions. Calming herself, she stepped onto the buggy. Jonathan set the horse in motion, and the pond finally faded in the distance. While the horse trotted softly through the snow, Jonathan slowed the pace. "You want to talk about it?"

Sophia never thought she would reveal her true feelings to anyone but Abigail, yet she felt she owed Jonathan an explanation. She told him the whole story, her feelings about Clayton, her insecurities, Mary's antics, even her own deceit.

"You are much too hard on yourself, Sophia," he reassured her. "If Clayton worried about the social differences, don't you think he would have given up on you when he found out the reason you lived on Park Lane?" he pointed out gently.

She hadn't thought of that. "He just doesn't know what's best for him."

"And you do?"

His words made her realize how motherly she sounded. "I just want him to be happy."

"I should think he would know what would make him happy better than anyone."

Sophia sniffed and wiped her tears with a mittened hand.

Jonathan sighed. "Look, you don't have to be a martyr. Let him make the choice."

A slight pause followed, as she seemed to consider his advice.

A rustling in the trees caught her attention. A tiny group of sparrows sought shelter from the biting cold between furry white branches. *They're just like me,* she thought. *I want to hide from the cold sting of Mary's cruel actions.*

Sophia drew in a long breath. The air smelled fresh and clean. She tried to relax as they traveled along the countryside. Her gaze lingered on spiraling smoke that curled from the distant chimneys of scattered farmhouses.

"Just think about it," Jonathan encouraged.

She turned to him. "You're a good friend, Jonathan. I'm thankful the Lord brought you here."

"I am too. And between you and me, I wish Abigail would hurry back." They laughed, and he tapped the reins, pushing the horses to a faster trot.

seventeen

That night, Clayton couldn't get Sophia off his mind. He pulled off his boots and let them drop to the floor. *When did she start seeing Jonathan? Why doesn't she give me a chance?* The questions haunted him.

He changed his clothes and finally crawled into bed. *Maybe she's just not interested in me.* Pride pricked him. *What about the way she looks at me? Doesn't it mean anything?* He stirred restlessly. *I'm probably just imagining it.* He pulled the thick covers over himself and punched his pillow into place.

One thing for sure, I'm not going to know how she feels if I don't spell out my feelings to her. I thought when I kissed her, she would know how I felt. He folded his pillow once more. *I'll never understand women.* He turned impatiently on his bed. *I will make my feelings known, and come what may, I'll deal with it. Anything is better than playing this game and not knowing.* His thoughts rambled, pushing sleep far from him.

Finally, he got up, reached into the trunk, and pulled out the journal. Somehow he felt better when he read through its pages.

February 12, 1867. It seems my temper always gets the better of me. I try to hold my tongue, but sometimes I feel it has a mind of its own. I think the Bible talks about it. Sometimes people are rude, and Mammá says I take it upon myself to put them in their places rather than letting God deal with them. I suppose it is true.

Tonight a boarder complained about Mammá's stew. A few of the tenants had not paid their rent, and Mammá

showed them kindness, giving them more time to pay. But
our finances have dwindled, and Mammá had little money
for stew meat. The boarder took a bite and barked, "Do
you call this stew, Woman? There's no meat in here!"

I looked at the tenants who had not paid, thinking they
would defend Mammá, but they kept silent. I suppose
they were afraid of the big bully, but I was not. I sat for a
full minute, trying to hold my tongue, but it was no use.
Before I knew it, I blurted out to him, "Mammá makes
the best stew of anyone. If you don't like it, go find yourself another place to grumble!"

I clamped my hand over my mouth as soon as the
words left me, but it was too late. The bully got up from
the table and shoved his chair out of the way, stomping
all the way down the hall.

I stood frozen in place, waiting for Mammá's wrath to
hurl down upon me, but she said nothing. The tenants
continued eating, while Mammá worked in the kitchen.

A few minutes later, the bully came out of his room
with a big bag across his shoulder. He slapped some
money on the table in front of Mammá and snapped,
"Here, now I'm up-to-date. I'm going where I can get a
decent meal." He turned and stomped out of the boardinghouse, slamming the door behind him.

I ran up the stairs to my room without dinner, knowing
it was my fault. Mammá came up a few minutes later
and sat on my bed. I wish she would have yelled at me,
but she didn't. She hugged me instead. She asked me if
the man's words hurt me. I told her yes.

She asked me, "Have Papá and I taught you to fight
hurt with hurt?"

I shook my head.

Her kind words echo in my heart still. "Remember,
Cara Mia, the book of Proverbs tells us a soft answer
turns away wrath." Sorrow chased my anger away, and I

*let Mammá know. I knew I had hurt her and hurt our
family business with my careless words. I caused a
boarder to leave, and we need boarders to survive.*

*She reminded me, "Lessons are worthwhile only if we
learn from them. I trust you will learn from this, Cara
Mia." She brushed the hair from my forehead and told
me to come downstairs before the stew got cold.*

*I went downstairs to eat. My actions hurt me even now
as I write this. I hope someday I will learn to control my
temper.*

Clayton closed the journal. Every entry revealed more insight to the writer's soul and stirred his heart to grow stronger
in his faith walk. Though he had given up on finding the
owner, he wished he could know her. But even more, he found
himself wishing he could know Sophia as intimately as he
knew the writer of the journal.

➳

Monday morning at the Relief Center, Martha Adams talked
excitedly about Mark Twain coming to town. "Oh, yes, Mr.
Twain will be speaking on Friday night," she informed all
who would listen. "He is a wonderful speaker, from what I
understand."

Sophia listened to the older woman, then watched as she
made her way to the next volunteer.

Sophia picked up the applications from her desk. The
dwindling stack before her proved many people had been
helped in the city, causing fewer people to come into the
Relief Center. Less pressure filled her days now that she
worked only a few hours a week at the center. It allowed her
more time to devote to her increasing sewing business.

"Hello, Sophia."

She looked up to see Clayton standing in front of her.
"Hello, Clayton." She thought of Jonathan's words. *Let him
make the choice.*

"Could I talk to you privately for a moment?"

She looked at him curiously. "Yes." She rose from her desk and followed him to a secluded corner behind two filing cabinets. She felt like a hammer was inside her chest, pounding to get out.

"Sophia, I know we've had some confusion between us, but, uh, I was wondering if we could put it behind us, and maybe—" Clayton stopped to clear his throat. "Would you consider going to hear Mark Twain with me on Friday night?" He stared deeply into her eyes.

Let him make the choice, Sophia. Jonathan's words echoed in her mind. "I'd be delighted, Clayton," she found herself saying.

He looked so surprised, Sophia had to look away momentarily to hide a chuckle. He took her hand and squeezed it. "I'll pick you up at seven o'clock, then?"

"Fine."

He bent next to her. "Thank you." His voice was low and tender.

Mrs. Adams opened the door to the center, signaling the start of another workday.

"I'd better get to my post," Sophia said, her heart in her throat.

Clayton held her hand a little longer than necessary. He reluctantly released his grasp. "Until Friday."

Sophia carried his words in her heart for the rest of the day, playing them over again and again.

❧

Mr. Twain's final comments left the audience laughing as they exited the building. "I can't recall when I've enjoyed myself so much," Sophia said with a merry heart.

Clayton helped her down the steps and into the carriage. She settled into her seat, smoothing her dress and cloak into place. They talked of their evening until the horses carried them down soft lamp-lit streets. Clayton pulled to the side of a less-traveled road. Sophia wondered what he was doing. She tried to swallow, but her throat turned dry as an empty well. Her fingers trembled beneath her gloves. He turned to face her.

"Sophia, you take my breath away." His whispered words made her shiver.

He looked intensely into her eyes. Brushing a stray hair from her face, he ran his fingers along the side of her cheek. Slowly, he lifted her chin toward him. His eyes fell upon her lips, and he leaned forward. At first his lips touched lightly upon hers. Stretching his arms around her, he embraced her gently, then pulled her closer to him, tighter. His lips pressed harder. The world seemed to pause in that moment. Nothing stirred. Anywhere. Her heart drummed strong, steady beats until she could scarcely breathe.

Clayton pulled away and looked at her. "I've been wanting to do that for a long time." She felt herself blush, then closed her eyes, not wanting the moment to end. He tenderly brought her next to him. They sat under the starlit skies for a moment or two.

With reluctance, Clayton guided the horses back onto the street, where they began a steady trot homeward. "I knew it could be like this," he said softly. Then he spoke abruptly as if a thought suddenly hit him. "Sophia, does this mean you're not as serious about Jonathan Clark as I feared?"

"Jonathan is merely a good friend and business associate. I suppose I could ask you the same about Mary Nottinger," she challenged, arching her brow.

He chuckled. "Mary and I are just friends. We grew up together. There's nothing to it. I take her out only as a friend." He squeezed her shoulder and looked at her for a long moment. "It's you I love, Sophia."

Sophia couldn't believe her ears. Did he say "love"?

The carriage drew to a stop in front of Mrs. Baird's house. Contentment settled upon her like a light airy breeze. She didn't want the night to end.

Clayton pulled her close and kissed her one last time. He helped Sophia out of the carriage and walked her to the door.

"Promise me we'll have many more evenings together like this one." His whispered words lingered in her ears. Clayton stared deep into her eyes.

She nodded shyly. He brushed a kiss on her forehead and whispered into her ear, "Until next time."

❧

On Monday morning, Abigail entered the shop in a whirl-wind, as always. "Good morning."

Sophia marveled her friend always wore a smile. She got up to greet her. "Abigail, how are you? I haven't seen you since your trip a week ago!"

Abigail pulled off her gloves. "Sophia, I know you're busy. Do you mind if I interrupt you for a short visit?"

Sophia thought of the hours of sewing awaiting her but replied, "Of course not. I want to hear all about your trip."

Abigail laughed, and the two made their way to the kitchen.

They spent the next hour discussing Abigail's trip and with Sophia telling of the events surrounding the ice-skating venture and her evening with Clayton.

"That's what happened," Sophia said matter-of-factly.

"Oh, you poor dear. How dreadful of Mary Nottinger! How can she be so cruel, so conniving, so—"

Sophia stopped her friend. "It doesn't matter. We had a wonderful evening listening to Mark Twain, and I think I'm finally working through our financial differences."

"Don't be a silly goose, Sophia. Clayton is not at all con-cerned with such things. Whatever made you think so?"

"Oh, I don't know." Sophia ran her finger along a line in the table.

"I'm glad you're finally seeing him for the wonderful man he truly is." Abigail looked at Sophia long and hard, then took a deep breath. "About your dress for the Christmas ball—"

"Oh, yes, I can't believe I forgot to tell you about it!" Sophia started to give her friend all the details of the dress pattern she had found when the bell on the front door echoed through the kitchen. Sophia got up in a hurry. "I'd better see who is here." Abigail nodded and reached for a couple of magazines on the table.

"Oh, there you are, my dear," said Alice Nottinger, as she pompously entered the room quite out of breath. "We were afraid you were closed."

"Hello, Mrs. Nottinger. Mary." Sophia's stomach twisted into knots.

"We came by to see how our dresses for the Christmas ball were coming along."

Sophia went over to a closet and pulled out the partially finished garments.

"Mary, what do you think, Dear?"

"I love it, Mother. Don't you just adore the red bow?"

"Oh, yes, quite."

Sophia stood to the side as they examined their garments.

"How lovely you will look standing alongside Clayton Hill. Why he will think you the belle of the ball in this dress, Mary," Mrs. Nottinger said, running her fingers across the lace, casting Sophia a sideways glance.

The comment sent pain rushing through Sophia.

"Are you going with Jonathan?" Mary asked, turning to Sophia.

It took Sophia a moment to find her voice. "I–I–I'm not sure I'll be attending after all."

"Oh?" Mary brought her hand to her mouth for dramatic emphasis. "It *would* be a shame if you didn't get to go, after preparing the dresses for all the prominent ladies in town."

Sophia's throat went dry.

"Mrs. Hill and I are the best of friends, you know," Mrs. Nottinger informed Sophia. "Have been for years. I suppose it's only natural for Mary and Clayton to one day be to-gether." Her words seemed to hold a warning. She turned and smiled at her daughter. "They are made for each other."

Mrs. Nottinger turned back to Sophia. "Mary would make a perfect wife for an attorney, don't you think?" Her eyes dared Sophia to contradict her.

Sophia began to gather the dresses. "I should have these ready for you by the middle of next week."

"That will be fine." Exaggerated sweetness thickened Mrs. Nottinger's voice.

"Mother, we'd best be going if I'm to meet Clayton for lunch." Mary looked at Sophia as if to make sure she had heard the last few words.

"Good day, Sophia," they said in unison.

Sophia stared after them as they exited the door.

Abigail, having heard everything, ran out to her friend who stood in a statuelike trance. "Sophia, are you all right?"

Abigail's words loosened Sophia from her shock. Sophia went back and forth with her feelings, while Abigail listened patiently. "They're absolutely right. I've been foolish to think I could fit in with any of them." Sophia was tired of trying. Mary had stripped away all of Sophia's self-confidence, and she could not muster the strength to get it back.

"Don't you dare listen to them, Sophia," Abigail admon-ished. "Don't you see it? They want to get you out of the way so Mary can have Clayton all to herself."

"She should have him. She's right for him. I'm tired of it all."

Abigail shook her head emphatically. "No! She is not right for him, and you know it. He is in love with you, Sophia. He even told you so. Why can't you believe him?"

"He's letting his heart rule. He needs to use common sense. His good judgment would tell him I'm wrong for him."

Abigail sighed. "I don't know what else to say, Sophia. I never thought you, of all people, would give up without a fight. I thought you said your father ingrained in you to never give up. I hope he can't see you now." Abigail let her words hang while she gathered her belongings. "I'll give you some time to yourself. I'm here for you when you need me." She patted Sophia on the shoulder and quietly left the shop.

eighteen

Sophia spent the next few weeks sewing furiously. Marie had finished her mending, so she started helping Sophia with the gowns. They finally finished each customer's Christmas dress for the ball.

Sophia's work at the Relief Center claimed the rest of her time, so she had few minutes to spare to think of Clayton. She had kept her distance from him since she found out he was taking Mary to the ball. Sophia explained to him how much work she had to do, and he seemed to understand and left her alone. Although no matter how hard she tried to keep him away, thoughts of him plagued her.

Sophia sighed as she placed the last finished garment in the narrow closet for customer pickup. The ball would be lovely, she was sure. She hoped Abigail would understand why she wasn't attending.

Bending over, Sophia blew out the lantern by the door. A tiny curl of smoke coiled from the wick. With a sigh, she looked into the darkness, then pulled the locked door softly behind her. This time, the tinkling bell did little to lift her spirits.

❧

"No, I do not understand, Sophia!" Abigail shook her head vigorously. Her hand thumped against the checkered tablecloth, causing the silverware to clatter. She briefly looked around the restaurant at the other patrons and lowered her voice. "You are my dearest friend in all the world, and you will not attend the biggest party I have ever given?" Genuine tears formed in Abigail's eyes as she pleaded with her friend. "Please, Sophia, you must come. You don't have to be around Mary and Clayton. I want you to be with me."

"You will be there with Jonathan. I will be out of place."

"Not true. Jonathan considers you a dear friend as well. We both want you there with us." Abigail grabbed her friend's hand. "Please, Sophia?"

"I'm sorry, Abigail, I just can't. Please forgive me." Sophia rose and left without finishing her lunch.

Stepping outside, Sophia glanced upward. An icy drizzle leaked from heavy gray clouds. "Perfect," Sophia fumed, pulling her bonnet farther over her forehead. She kicked a pebble in her path, her mood darkening with every step.

I'm upsetting everyone these days. Maybe I should move, make a new life for myself somewhere else. She sighed. *No, I couldn't leave Mammá.* The cold drizzle irritated her beyond belief. She pushed another stone aside with the toe of her shoes. *How could I hurt my best friend like that? None of this is Abigail's fault. Yet, how can I bear to watch Mary at the ball with Clayton?*

When she finally reached Mrs. Baird's house, she stepped through the door, allowing it to close with ample force. Silence met her. Shivering slightly from her wet wraps, Sophia pulled off her cloak. She placed her heavy garment in the hall closet, then quickly made her way up the stairs toward her room.

Once in her room, Sophia threw herself onto the bed. She felt miserable and quickly gave in to her feelings.

"Sophia, is that you, Dear?" Mammá called outside the bedroom. Before Sophia could collect her voice, her mother tapped on the door.

Sophia's muffled cries filled the room. Mammá tiptoed inside. She sat down beside her daughter, brushing the hair back from the side of her face. *"Cara Mia,* what is troubling you?"

Sophia sobbed a few moments more, while her mother waited patiently.

"Oh, Mammá, I have made such a mess of everything,"

she finally said, pulling herself up. Her tear-stained face met her mother's kind gaze.

"How have you done so?"

"Abigail is mad at me because I won't go to the Christmas ball, and—"

Her mother interrupted. "Not go to the ball? And why not, Sophia?" Her mother's eyes were large, curious.

"I can't go, Mammá, not with Clayton and Mary there and me without an escort."

Her mother waved her hand. "Never would Papá believe his daughter would give up so easily. No, he would not hear of such a thing. You must go. You are strong. The Lord will help you through this. You need to go for Abigail," her mother admonished.

"And what about me, Mammá? What about my feelings?" The moment she said the words, she heard the self-pity in them and felt ashamed.

"*Cara Mia,* I have never known you to put yourself before others."

Sophia lowered her head. Mammá cupped and lifted Sophia's chin. "God will go with you, my dear daughter. You hold your head high and be a good friend."

Wiping her nose once more on her handkerchief, Sophia struggled with feelings of pride and anger. She knew her mother was right about being a good friend, but Sophia didn't know if she could face everyone at the ball. Her mother wisely waited, allowing Sophia to work through her inner turmoil.

She thought of her papá and his strong resolve to keep others first, no matter what the cost. His godly example gave her the strength she needed.

She quieted her last sniffle. "You are right," she whispered, drawing on new strength. "I don't know how I will do it, but I will go, Mammá."

Her mother patted her hand. "God will guide you. You will see."

Sophia's eyes grew wide. "Oh, my, I don't have a dress, and the ball is next Monday!"

"I will watch the shop for you while you prepare your dress. You can do this?"

Sophia thought for a minute. With the Christmas gowns finished, there would not be much sewing to do in the next week. She bit her lip. "Yes, Mammá, I can do this."

❧

"I will tell Miss Mary you are here," the butler said as he led Clayton into the parlor.

Clayton settled onto the settee. The cushion was stiff. He tried to get comfortable, but it was no use. He glanced around. The straight-backed chairs across from him didn't appear any more inviting. The room felt cold, sterile. Funny, he had never noticed that before. He sighed and glanced at his pocket watch.

"Well, Clayton, what do you think?" Mary asked as she entered the room with her Christmas gown.

Clayton thought her voice arrogant and irritating. "Your dress is very nice, Mary. I'm sorry to be in such a hurry, but I really must be going," he said, rising. "I only stopped over to return the parasol you left in my carriage." He made every effort to be patient.

Mary followed him into the hallway. "Aren't you going to ask me?" She stomped her foot against the marble flooring.

"Ask you what?" He was growing impatient with her childish behavior.

"You haven't asked me to the ball yet, Clayton. I've turned down other offers, feeling sure you would get around to it soon; but frankly, Clayton, I'm tired of waiting." She extended her lower lip and fluttered her eyelashes.

He hadn't noticed how ridiculous these actions made her look until now. Usually this tactic made him feel guilty and caused him to give in to her wants—but not this time. "I'm sorry if I've misled you, Mary, but I had no intention of asking you." He didn't mean for the words to sound so harsh.

Her face began to contort. "I suppose you're planning to take Sophia Martone," she spat. "She has nothing to offer you. Poor little seamstress."

He watched, speechless, as venom continued to spew from her lips. Was this his friend from school days? He'd never seen this side of her before.

"Oh, she could tailor a suit for you, perhaps, to wear to a Sunday social. She could embarrass you in her peasant frocks at the business gatherings—"

"Enough! I will hear no more!" His sharp words silenced her tongue at once. "I know, Mary, our families have been close since our childhood, and I've tried to show you respect because of that. But I've had quite enough of your antics!" He turned toward the front door and grabbed the handle.

"Oh, that's right, Clayton. Let's not tarnish your dear little Sophia—"

He turned to face Mary. Preparing to defend Sophia, he remembered the journal entry. What was it, something about "a soft answer turns away wrath"? He swallowed the ugly words that waited in his throat.

Mary continued, "Who, by the way, happens to be in love with Jonathan Clark."

Her words seared his heart like a hot iron. He prayed she wasn't right.

"My poor, dear, Clayton. Your true love is in love with another. Are you sure you want to ask her to the ball and be turned down flat?"

Her words took the fight out of him in one single blow. "It's a chance I'm willing to take, Mary." He turned and quietly walked out the front door.

❧

The next few days at the Relief Center, Clayton felt as though he needed to avoid Sophia for reasons he didn't understand. He thought their evening out to hear Mark Twain offered a new beginning for their relationship. Yet things ended where they had started. He wondered what went wrong. In spite of her cold treatment of him, he watched her reach out in kindness to those in need, and his love for her grew stronger. How could he go on like this?

Maybe Mary was right. Maybe Sophia did love Jonathan Clark. She said they were friends, but Clayton realized she'd never really answered his question that night in the carriage. Still, she had kissed him. Could she kiss him with such tenderness if she were in love with someone else?

Clayton stumbled through the following days, barely speaking with Sophia, though he longed to talk with her, to hold her once again. Nothing made sense to him anymore.

Their work at the center grew easier. With Christmas fast approaching, most families had settled into temporary shanties and came into the center mainly for food.

Sophia's voice interrupted his thoughts. "Merry Christmas," she called to the remaining workers before she exited the building.

Clayton grabbed his coat and quickly ran out the door after her. He had to find out if what Mary said was true.

He noticed Mr. Higgins wasn't waiting for Sophia. Was she walking all the way back? He thought she had learned the dangers of walking alone the night she met Jake Elders.

Slightly out of breath, he finally reached her. "Sophia?"

She turned around to face him. "Hello, Clayton," she said with the tone of a casual acquaintance.

"Is Mr. Higgins driving you tonight?" he asked, his breath escaping in hazy puffs.

She lowered her eyelids. "No, he has fallen ill, I'm afraid." As she turned she added, "I'm sorry, I must be going. It will be dark soon." Her steps continued at a quickened pace.

Clayton could bear it no longer. He had to know what was going on, and he had to know now! "Sophia." He touched her arm. She stopped and turned to face him once again. Her eyes looked like dark, shimmering pools in which he could get lost.

"Please, let me take you home." His voice was soft, pleading.

She bit her lip. "I don't know. . . ."

"Please."

"If you're sure you want to."

He touched her elbow to guide her through the snow. "Sophia, why wouldn't I want to?"

She didn't answer.

They reached his carriage, and he helped her up. He climbed aboard beside her. The snow fell gently around them as his horses' hooves crunched into heavy, white mounds. The evening air grew chilly, but not bitterly cold. Clayton pushed the buffalo skin closer to Sophia.

"Thank you," she said with a warm smile.

They continued on as stars twinkled against the dusky sky. Clayton glanced at the homes along the way. Kerosene lanterns glowed from window frames as families gathered for dinner. Curly, gray smoke puffed from brick chimneys, filling the night air with the pleasant scent of burning wood. They rode awhile in silence.

"Do you mind if I stop at the post office?" Clayton asked as they drew near the building.

"No, of course not."

"I'll only be a minute." He quickly hopped out of the carriage.

Keeping true to his word, he came back shortly. He climbed back in and impatiently urged the horses back on the path.

"Is something wrong?"

"Oh, I'm frustrated. I have something that belongs to someone else, and I'm trying to find the owner." He turned the corner. "I've put an ad in the paper several different times, hoping for a response, but the ad's finally run out, and still no news."

"Oh, I'm sorry." Her eyelids fell, brushing soft snowflakes against her face.

"Wasn't meant to be, I guess. At least I tried."

"That's too bad. I know what it's like to lose something important."

He wondered what she had lost but decided against asking. She might not like it if he asked too many questions. He didn't want to upset her now that she was finally talking to him again.

"Are you excited about Christmas?" He wanted to change the subject.

"Yes." Her words held little enthusiasm.

"I suppose you and Jonathan are going to the ball?" He hoped his voice didn't reveal his fear.

"No, I'm going to the ball alone." Sophia kept her eyes fixed on the road.

"Alone? Why?" He turned to face her.

"Because I–I—well, I just am, that's all." She pulled impatiently at her buffalo skin.

"That makes two of us."

"What?" She turned a surprised look to him.

He shrugged. "Whom would I take? The only woman I want beside me is you, and I thought you were going with Jonathan. I was certain you wouldn't go with me."

Sophia sat speechless for a moment. "But I–I thought you were taking Mary Nottinger."

"Where did you ever get an idea like that, Sophia?" His words were heavy with feeling. "I've told you before, Mary and I are just friends. We always have been, we always will be."

"But she told me. . ." Sophia let the words drift with the falling snow.

He pulled to the side of the road and boldly grabbed her right hand, looking straight into her eyes. "Look, Sophia, I don't know where all these misunderstandings have come from, but something tells me Mary Nottinger is behind all of this."

She looked away.

"Please, Sophia, I have to know why you keep pulling away from me."

She lowered her shoulders and exhaled. "All right, I will tell you." Taking another deep breath, she began, "We're not right for each other, Clayton. You are—you are—you are wealthy and we, my mother and I, have very little. We only live in a beautiful house because Mrs. Baird took pity on us. That's why I didn't tell you where I lived—because I was ashamed." She drew in a long breath and continued before she lost her nerve. "You belong with someone of your kind, someone like. . .Mary Nottinger." She lowered her gaze as tears slid down her cheeks and plopped onto the buffalo skin.

His body stiffened. "What? Is that why you've been ignoring me? Because you decided you weren't good enough, because you decided I belonged with Mary?" His voice rose with every word. He stared at her. "Mary planted those thoughts in your head!" He hit his gloved hand on the carriage seat.

Sophia sat silently.

He grabbed both of her hands now. "Sophia, please look at me." His words were soft, inviting. She lifted her head, meeting his gaze.

"That means nothing to me. You are the woman I love. I've known that for a long time. I don't know if you could ever feel the same, but—"

Sophia stopped his words. Slipping her right hand from his, she placed the tips of her fingers against his mouth to silence him. Her eyes locked with his, and he felt his heart would stop beating. "I do feel the same, Clayton. I love you too."

Enveloped in the night shadows, Clayton pulled her into the circle of his arms and placed a slow, thoughtful kiss upon her lips.

Her nearness made his senses spin. His heart jolted and his pulse pounded as her lips surrendered to his kiss. Did she really say she loved him? He pulled away and looked into her eyes once more. Her dark brown eyes hinted of soft velvet. A shy smile etched the corners of Sophia's mouth before she turned away.

"One more thing." He let out a slight cough. "Will you go to the ball with me?"

Sparkling eyes met his. "I would love to go with you, Clayton."

He pulled her into his arms again and held her tight. When he released her, Clayton returned his attention to the horses, gently leading them toward home. He could hardly speak, his heart was so full. His thoughts darted in every direction. He couldn't wait to tell everyone the news. Sophia loved him! He wanted to shout it into the dusky night, still he held himself in check, hoping the noisy *clip-clop* of the horses would rise above the thumping of his heart.

As they continued on the road, Sophia broke the silence. "I want to apologize, Clayton, for my deceit. It was wrong, and I'm sorry."

"Look, Sophia, we've both made some mistakes. Thankfully, it's all behind us now, right?"

She nodded with a smile. "I'm glad you brought me home tonight," Sophia said as he pulled up to Mrs. Baird's home. "It makes Christmas more bearable this year."

He lifted her chin to look at him. "Why is Christmas so hard?"

Sophia shrugged slightly and lowered her head. "We lost a special family trunk in the fire. Papá had bought it for Mammá when we moved here from Italy. It has been our family tradition for Mammá to pull out the trunk each year at Christmas, where it sets beside the tree and holds our presents in safekeeping." She paused for a moment, then looked at him. "Papá died in 1866, did I ever tell you that?"

Clayton shook his head.

"In the cholera epidemic. Mammá still pulled out the trunk

at Christmastime, even after Papá died, but not this year. This is our first Christmas without the trunk."

Clayton's mind reeled as he began to fit the pieces together. The writer and Sophia both loved sleigh rides, they both had to learn English, they both were encouraged to dream. Was it possible that he read nightly from Sophia's journal that had been tucked away in her treasured trunk? His hands felt sweaty, his heart raced.

He couldn't tell her. . .not yet.

nineteen

The week before Christmas found Sophia engulfed in a flurry of activities. Her mother watched the shop as Sophia worked with diligence to get her dress made on time.

When Sophia finished the final stitch, she stood and shook out her dress, allowing the soft velvet to cascade to the floor in a delicate sweep. She held it in front of her and gazed upon it in the looking glass. "Mammá, it's finished!"

Her mother turned, clutching her hand to her chest. "Sophia, you must not startle me so," she said as she stepped from behind the counter toward her daughter.

"I'm sorry, Mammá. I couldn't help myself."

At first sight of the gown, her mother gasped. "*Cara Mia,* it is beautiful." She ran her fingers lightly along the front of the material. "And you still have two days until Christmas!" She smiled.

Together they looked upon the green velvet. "Mrs. Baird's emerald necklace, that she insists upon you wearing, will look beautiful against the scooped neck. You will look like a princess, Sophia." Her mother brushed her fingers against Sophia's cheek.

"Thank you, Mammá."

The two discussed the dress and what accessories Sophia would wear with it the night of the ball.

When Abigail entered the shop, she let out a squeal. "Who gets to wear that?" Her eyes grew wide with admiration.

Sophia smiled. "It's my gown for the ball."

"Sophia, you will look charming." Abigail hugged her best friend. "Clayton will be totally smitten!"

They laughed together and talked about their upcoming

plans. The front door bell jangled once more, pulling them from their conversation.

Mary Nottinger stepped through the entrance. She lifted her chin. Her words were cold and formal. "Sophia, I'm afraid you'll have to mend a seam on my dress for the Christmas ball. There seems to be a tear."

"Oh? I'm sorry. Let me take a look at it." Sophia placed her own gown on the counter and reached for Mary's.

Mary handed the garment to her.

Sophia studied the tear and noted the material was ripped in an area away from the seam. She puzzled at this. No doubt Mary carelessly tried it on and the material ripped when she removed the dress. Fortunately, the tear was under a ruffle and could be easily mended.

Mary looked at the dress draped over the counter. "Oh my, whose marvelous gown is this?" Without permission, she lifted the delicate velvet and felt the soft cloth with her fingers.

Abigail looked at Mammá, and before either could respond, Sophia interjected, "That is my gown for the ball, Mary."

Mary turned to her with a start. "I thought you weren't going. Did you change your mind?" Her voice was curt and challenging.

"Yes, I did." Sophia felt heat climb her cheeks.

"Are you going with Jonathan?" She said it more as a demand than a question.

"No, actually, Abigail is going with Jonathan."

Mary turned calculating eyes toward Abigail, then back to Sophia. "And you, whom are you going with?"

"I will be attending the ball with Clayton." Sophia tried to speak gently. Despite Mary's conniving, Sophia really did not want to hurt her.

"Oh, I see." Mary dropped the dress back onto the counter. The gown started to slide off when Mammá caught it and carefully placed the velvet back into place.

"I will send our driver back tomorrow morning for my

gown," Mary called as she quickly exited, leaving no room for Sophia to respond. "I trust you are capable of mending it." Mary reached the door, then turned back toward Sophia. "It will be nice to have you at the ball. In case my dress should happen to rip again, you'll be close by to mend it. See you there." A wicked smirk spread across her face, making Sophia uneasy.

The door slammed to a close. The three stood in silence. Abigail was the first to speak. "Did you see that? She turned as green as your dress!" Abigail's eyes flashed with delight.

"I don't like it. I don't like it at all." Mammá shook her head.

Sophia knew her mother had seen it too. Mary's eyes, her expression, something chilled Sophia to the bone.

"What is it, Mammá?"

"She means trouble, *Cara Mia*. We must pray for Mary." Concern filled every word.

Sophia attempted to shake off her misgivings. She wanted to be happy and rid herself of Mary Nottinger's scheming once and for all.

"Mammá, Clayton has asked me to go to the Christmas ball with him. My dress is ready, and the ball is only two days away. What could go wrong?"

Mammá said nothing. She looked at her daughter, then stared toward the door, her brows knitted into a frown.

"Enough worry. Let me put this away. We all need to go home for dinner. I'm starving," Sophia said with a forced laugh. Taking her dress from the counter, she placed it in the closet.

Abigail and Mammá put on their coats and went outside. Sophia pulled on her cloak and took one last look at her gown. Her mother's words echoed in her mind, and Sophia prayed there would be no more trouble from Mary Nottinger.

❧

On Christmas Eve, the smell of roasted turkey filled Mrs. Baird's house while Sophia busied herself in the kitchen, folding napkins, rearranging the silver, and placing spoons in large serving bowls.

"Sophia, calm yourself, or you'll be exhausted by the time the Hills arrive," Mammá said as she walked over and gave her daughter a hug. "The table looks beautiful, *Cara Mia.*" They looked together at the Rose Canton china and flickering candles nestled between thick greenery laced with velvety red ribbons. The golden turkey sat in the middle of the table, along with potatoes, bowls of sweet pickles, jewel-toned jellies, and tender persimmons prepared with cinnamon and brown sugar. Spicy fruitcakes, dried chestnuts, and plum pudding would complete the meal.

Sophia grabbed her mother's hand and pulled her into the sitting room, where candles flickered against the walls, the hearth held an enormous fire that blazed up the chimney, and thick cords of greenery hugged the arched doorway and windows. The far corner was empty, cleared for the tree that Clayton would be bringing. Stockings hung across the mantel, bulging with apples and oranges, walnuts, and homemade caramels.

A large crock contained yards of popcorn strung for the tree. Waiting to be uncurled, tiny paper chains huddled in a small box. Mrs. Baird brought out some heirloom glass balls in glittering colors.

Sophia felt her heart quicken when she heard Clayton and his parents enter the house, thumping snow from their shoes. She squared her shoulders and stepped forward. From sheer happiness, she felt sure she glowed like a glass ornament.

❧

Scents of dinner lingered and meandered through the sitting room, joining the aroma of hot cider. The fireplace warmed the room as the small group sat contentedly in the silence.

Clayton secretly ran his fingers tenderly along Sophia's hand. She met his gaze and reveled in the love she saw there.

Sophia's eyes grew sleepy as she sat next to Clayton with the soft firelight and the beautifully decorated tree before them.

"Why did your parents leave so soon?" Sophia asked.

"They always retire early," he said, "but I know they had a wonderful time."

Mrs. Baird placed her novel on the stand and yawned.

Mammá looked up from her mending.

Clayton didn't want to overstay his welcome. "I'd better be going."

Clayton stood as Mammá and Mrs. Baird prepared to retire for the evening. Each one expressed her delight in the wonderful evening and said her good nights.

Sophia walked Clayton to the door.

"I'll miss you in the morning, but tomorrow night at the Christmas ball, you'll belong to me," he whispered. "I can hardly wait to share the evening with you."

"Me too," she said softly, leaning lightly against his chest.

"Oh, I almost forgot," he said as he fumbled around in his pocket and pulled out some mistletoe.

Sophia saw it and laughed.

"What? It's a little scrawny, but it's still useable." He looked to make sure no one was around. Then he held it over their heads with one arm, and with the other, he pulled Sophia to him and brushed his warm lips over hers, making a myriad of colors and lights flash under her closed eyes.

She gently pulled away. "Good night, Clayton."

"Good night, Sophia. I love you."

twenty

The bright morning sun streamed into Sophia's window, announcing the glorious news that Christmas had arrived. Realizing she had overslept, she quickly pulled on her clothes. With hurried sweeps, she brushed through her hair, not taking time to pin it up but rather allowing it to fan across her shoulders.

She glanced out the window and saw a thick blanket of snow stretched across the lawn and heaps of white weighing down tree branches and bushes. Excitement surged through her.

She ran down the stairs to the sitting room, where her mother and Mrs. Baird sat casually sipping hot tea. The warmth of the fireplace greeted her when she entered the room. "I'm sorry. I didn't realize you were waiting on me."

"Nonsense, Dear. Get some tea and join us." Mrs. Baird smiled, rocking happily in her chair.

Sophia nodded, then poured her drink. She sat down with her tea and looked at the tree. Despite the beautiful decorations they placed on it the night before, she couldn't help thinking something was missing.

Mammá caught her daughter's expression. "I know, *Cara Mia*. It looks different without the trunk."

Sophia nodded sadly. "I fear Christmas will never be the same."

Silence hung in the air.

Mrs. Baird's voice interrupted their despair. "It's still Christmas, ladies, and we will not be sad today," she announced as she passed around some sugary rolls.

Sophia had just taken a bite when a soft knock sounded from the front door.

Mammá looked at Mrs. Baird. "Who would be calling on Christmas morning?"

Mrs. Baird shrugged. "Perhaps I should go see," she said with a hint of amusement in her voice.

Sophia and her mother waited in the sitting room as Mrs. Baird answered the door.

"Come on in," she said to her visitors. "We're in the sitting room."

"Well, look who's come calling on Christmas Day," Mrs. Baird announced with a wide grin.

"Clayton!" Sophia almost bolted from the chair, then remembered her manners and took even steps across the floor. She stopped when she saw Clayton and his father heaving a large blanket-wrapped item into the room. Mrs. Hill followed closely behind.

Sophia wondered what mischief Clayton was up to. Childhood excitement rushed through her. She had always liked surprises as a little girl. The end result never mattered to her. It was the secrecy surrounding the gift that delighted her.

The two men gently lowered their mysterious load to the floor. Clayton brushed his hands together and looked into her puzzled face. "All right if we have some tea?"

Before she could respond, Mrs. Baird chimed in, "Of course. Let me take your wraps. So glad you could join us." Her words trailed to quiet mumbles as they followed her into another room.

They quickly returned, allowing Sophia and her mother no time to discuss the surprise visit. Upon entering, Mr. and Mrs. Hill gave their Christmas greetings. They spoke of the wonderful dinner the night before and the uncertainty of the winter weather.

Sophia talked politely and slid a glance over to Clayton, who was staring at her. Their eyes locked. His expression held a secret.

She bit her lip. Her gaze went from Clayton to the hidden

box, then back to Clayton.

His elusive smile stayed in place.

Mrs. Baird came back into the room, and everyone sat comfortably around the tree and the mysterious box.

Sophia wondered what was happening. Mrs. Baird hadn't told her the Hills were coming today. She ran her hand absently along her hair, then flushed when she remembered it was hanging across her shoulders. She wished she had known so she could have dressed more appropriately.

Clayton's eyes crinkled with amusement. He looked at Sophia and her mother. "You're probably wondering why we're here."

They both nodded. Sophia wanted to hug him and poke him all at the same time. Couldn't he tell how anxious they were? She wished he'd hurry up with the explanation.

"It's a long story, which I'll be happy to tell you later, but right now I want to present you with a special Christmas gift." Clayton rose from his chair and walked over to the blanket-covered bundle.

Sophia and her mother exchanged a curious look.

The room fell silent as Clayton peeled away the layers of blankets and stepped away.

Sophia felt her smile fade as disbelief sent shock running through every nerve in her body. Tears blinded her eyes and choked her voice as she numbly made her way to their family's precious trunk.

Mammá gasped, bringing both hands to her face. *"Cara Mia*, Papá's trunk!" she cried, tears running down her cheeks.

Trembling, Sophia knelt down and embraced the trunk. Mammá went over beside her. Together, they ran their fingers across the lid and sides, crying tears of joy.

Sophia noticed how pleasure shone from the faces of the guests and the hostess as they watched her and Mammá get reacquainted with an old friend.

The room grew quiet with the poignancy of the moment.

Sophia wiped the tears from her face and looked at her mother. Mammá's head was bowed. A hushed prayer lingered on her lips. Finally, she turned her red face to her daughter. "Papá is still with us, *Cara Mia.*" She grabbed Sophia's hand and squeezed it.

"How? Where?" she could barely whisper as she looked at Clayton. "Is this what you were trying to match with its owners?"

He nodded.

She got up and went to him. Looking down, she twisted the handkerchief in her hand, then looked into his face. "Thank you, Clayton." Her words were barely audible.

"You're welcome," he said quietly.

As the excitement of the moment swept over her, she impulsively grabbed his arm and gave it a happy tug. "How did you know? Where did you find it?" Questions tumbled out one after the other. He laughed heartily, then finally explained the story.

Mammá appeared lost in thought, staring at the trunk, dabbing tears with her handkerchief.

Mrs. Hill got up and hugged her. "I'm so happy you have found your trunk at last."

Mr. Hill followed behind his wife and expressed his joy to Mammá.

Mrs. Baird called to the cheerful crowd, "Are you going to carry on all day, or are we going to get to enjoy Christmas?"

They all laughed.

Finally, they sat down once again and faced the tree. Clayton spoke. "I've got a confession to make."

Sophia looked at him curiously.

"I hope you don't mind, Sophia, but I read your journals."

She gasped.

"Of course, at the time, I didn't know they belonged to you," he quickly added.

She relaxed a little.

"It did give me insight into your Christmas tradition. For now, I have placed your treasured belongings safely in a box, which I will present to you shortly, but your mother has graciously consented to allow me to pass out gifts this year." He looked at Mammá, and she gave him a wink.

Sophia placed her trembling hands in her lap and smiled at him.

Slowly, Christmas treasures were pulled from the trunk—a delicate shawl, hand-knit gloves, and a leather-bound journal, to name a few, until everyone had received a carefully chosen gift. When it seemed the gift giving was over, Mrs. Baird called Mammá and the Hills to the kitchen, mumbling something about fruitcake.

Clayton called Sophia over to kneel beside him and the trunk.

Once Sophia joined him, Clayton began to speak. "It seems I've left one gift behind." He took in a ragged breath. "I'd like for you to pull it out, please."

Sophia wondered what could be left. She opened the lid and gently lifted out a small box. Carefully opening it, her eyes fell upon a delicate gold band with a solitary, glistening diamond. Her mouth dropped open and a soft gasp escaped. At what moment did she step into this perfect world? "Clayton, it's beautiful!"

Clayton took it from her hands and faced her. He looked into her eyes. "Sophia Martone, I love you, and I want to spend the rest of my life with you." He paused, as if gathering courage. "Will you marry me?"

Her heart pounded in her ears as though it would burst. Nothing in all her life had compared to the happiness she felt at this moment. "Oh, yes, Clayton, I will marry you."

Grasping her left hand, he placed the ring on her trembling finger, then pulled her into a warm embrace. Sophia breathed a prayer of thanksgiving as she rested in the arms of the man she loved.

The rest of the group finally entered, and the room was filled with congratulations and hugs.

When the excitement settled down, Mammá spoke up. "I don't mean to rush you, Dear, but you need to pick up your gown from the shop."

Sophia sat up straight, pulling her hands to her face. "Oh, I almost forgot!"

"Would you like me to take you?" Clayton asked.

"Oh, no, I don't want you to see the dress until tonight."

"My driver is off for Christmas, but I believe I can still move a carriage," Mrs. Baird said with a chuckle, delighted with herself.

"I will come too," Mammá joined in.

"It's time for us to go home so these two lovebirds can prepare for their big night," Mrs. Hill said, making her rounds with hugs.

With all the good-byes completed, Clayton and Sophia stood alone in the doorway. He held her hands as his eyes lingered on her face. "I can hardly wait until tonight, my love." He placed a light kiss upon her forehead and turned toward the carriage. "The ball starts at nine o'clock, so I'll pick you up at eight thirty," he called with a final wave.

Sophia waved and reluctantly closed the door, fearing she was caught up in a beautiful dream.

twenty-one

"I'll only be a minute," Sophia said. She climbed from the carriage and headed toward the front door of her shop. With a gentle push, she opened the door. Instantly, an icy chill rippled up her spine. She wondered why. This shop was practically her second home. Why would she suddenly feel afraid? She struggled to shake the uneasiness.

"This is silly," she said out loud as she worked her way through the shop. When she walked into the back room to check on things, she noticed the air was a bit cool. Throwing a quick glance at the back door, she felt her throat constrict. She stood still for a moment before she took a deep breath and went over to inspect the partially opened door. Though only cracked open, the wisp of a draft slipped through to nip the air.

She thought she had locked it the night before. She normally did that as a matter of routine, but had she forgotten? What if someone had tried to get in? Who would want to get into her store? Why? The business held nothing of real value—no cash, just bolts of cloth. Sophia quietly closed the door, then locked it. She pulled on it to make sure it stayed locked.

After tiptoeing around the shop and peering into dark corners, Sophia found nothing missing. She finally convinced herself that in all the Christmas excitement, she must have left the door unlocked. She felt herself calming.

"Sophia, is everything all right?" Mammá asked as she and Mrs. Baird entered the door, both looking concerned.

"I'm sorry. Yes, everything's fine. I just noticed the back door was ajar, and I thought I should take a look around."

"Oh, dear," Mammá exclaimed, quickly scanning the room.

"Don't worry, Mammá, everything is in place."

"You're sure, Sophia?" Mrs. Baird asked in a motherly tone.

"Yes." Sophia assured them, resigning herself to the fact that she now had two mothers to watch over her. "Just let me get my dress, and we can go."

"How do you suppose that happened, Sophia?" Mammá asked while she and Mrs. Baird walked toward the front door.

Sophia walked over to the closet. "Oh, I don't know, Mammá. I suppose in all the Christmas excitement, I just—" Sophia let out a gasp.

Mammá and Mrs. Baird jerked around to face her.

"What is it?" Mrs. Baird asked as they ran to Sophia's side.

"My dress—it's gone."

❧

Mrs. Baird closed the closet door, while Mammá attempted to soothe Sophia. "It makes no sense, no sense at all," Mrs. Baird said, shaking her head. "Who would want your dress, Sophia?"

Mammá looked at Sophia. *"Cara Mia."* Her eyes stretched wide, her face revealing a suspicion.

"What is it, Mammá?"

Mammá grabbed her hand. "Do you think Mary Nottinger—"

"Oh, no, Mammá. Even Mary would not do such a thing as this." Sophia refused to believe Mary could be that cruel. Still, doubts began to flood her mind.

Mammá waved her hand. "No matter. We must get you another dress."

"It's not possible, Mammá. All the stores are closed, even if we had the money, which we do not, and there's certainly no time to make another one." Light tears splashed from Sophia's cheeks onto the floor. "No, I'm afraid I will not be attending the ball tonight."

"Papá said, 'Never give up,' Sophia." Mammá lifted Sophia's chin and looked into her eyes. "You believe, *Cara Mia?* Hmm? You believe God will see you through this?"

Sophia's tears had diminished to a lone trickle. She answered halfheartedly, "Yes, I believe."

Her mother motioned for Mrs. Baird to join them in a circle. "Hold hands," Mammá instructed.

"Dear Father," she began.

Sophia and Mrs. Baird quickly bowed their heads.

"You see our need. You say we are to give all our cares to You because You care about us. We believe it is true. We know things don't always work out the way we plan, but we believe You are always with us, and You bring joy to us even through the disappointments of life. Help Sophia, Father. Just when this wonderful thing has happened that Clayton proposes to her, this sad thing has happened with her dress. We don't know who took it, Father, but You know. Help that person to come to You. We forgive them, even though we are still sorry this thing has happened. Give us joy today, Father, for this is the day You have made. In Jesus' name," and all three said in unison, "Amen."

"Thank you, Mammá," Sophia whispered, giving her mother a hug.

"It will work out, *Cara Mia,* you will see."

Sophia silently wished she had her mother's strong faith. In the midst of her own struggles, Sophia sometimes found it difficult to believe things would all work out. Yet her mother's sincere prayer had given her renewed hope. She didn't know if she would be going to the ball but knew God would help her through it. Still, the disappointment sank deep into her soul.

Once they were home, Sophia quickly went up the stairs to her room and closed the door. She needed time to be alone and think about things. She glanced at the clock on the table. The ball was set to start in six hours. She wanted to go to bed and sleep through it so she didn't have to feel the ache that grew within her.

"Enough," she told herself. "I'm behaving like a child."

Sophia walked over to her washbasin and poured some water from the pitcher into the bowl. She grabbed a cloth and wiped her face. With a glance in the looking glass, she nodded sharply. "I will be fine." She refused to give in to self-pity anymore.

"Sophia," her mother called from downstairs.

Sophia opened her door and went to the top of the stairs, "Yes, Mammá?" Just as Sophia spotted her mother, she saw Abigail standing beside her.

Abigail ran up the stairs. "Sophia, I ran into Clayton this morning just after he left your house. He told me the news! Congratulations!" Abigail threw her arms around her friend with so much force, Sophia feared they would fall down the stairs. She laughed in spite of herself.

"We had better move away from the stairway," Sophia said as she attempted to hold her balance.

Abigail chuckled as they went to the landing. "Sorry. I can't help it. I am so happy for you." She pulled off her bonnet and straightened her hair. "Sophia, are you going to show me the ring?"

"Oh, yes," she said as she extended her hand.

"My goodness, it's absolutely beautiful, Sophia." Abigail hugged her once more. "Imagine," she said longingly as she held her hand against her heart, "being engaged to be married." She let out a long sigh.

"Abby, you are so dramatic."

"What?" Abigail looked at her incredulously. "Aren't you thrilled beyond words? I would be dancing on the roof if I were you!" she said as she pulled off her gloves. "Oh, no matter, you'll be dancing together soon enough at the ball. And I can see Mary Nottinger's face now!" A big grin stretched across Abigail's face until she looked at Sophia. "What is it? What's wrong?"

"Right now, I don't see how I can go to the ball, Abigail. I haven't even told Clayton yet."

Abigail grabbed Sophia's shoulders. "What? You're not going? Why?"

"It's a long story." Sophia was hoping to get out of an explanation, but she knew better.

"I have time," Abigail said, walking over to the top step, sitting down and patting a seat beside her.

Sophia sighed, then settled beside her friend, explaining the whole story of the missing dress.

After hearing the story, Abigail shot up from the stairway and began putting on her coat.

Puzzled, Sophia asked, "Where are you going?"

"I'll be back, Sophia."

"But—"

"I'll talk to you later," she called out as she practically ran down the steps and out the door.

With mouth gaping, Sophia watched her leave the house. She couldn't imagine why Abigail reacted that way. Didn't she even care that Sophia couldn't go? Maybe Abby had to tend to something, her hair perhaps, and didn't have the time to explain. Sophia couldn't worry about that. She had enough things to think about already.

"Would you care to join us for tea?" her mother called from the sitting room. Sophia slipped in to join them. Her mother was already pouring the hot liquid into cups.

"You told Abigail about the dress?" Mammá asked.

Sophia nodded.

Mrs. Baird shook her head. "Poor dear." She clicked her tongue before taking a sip of tea.

"I must get word to Clayton, or he will expect me to be ready tonight when he arrives." Sophia nervously bit her lip.

"We must not lose faith," Angelica encouraged. She sat down beside the fireplace.

"But what if—"

"Sophia, if Clayton comes and you are not prepared for the ball, he can take you to dinner instead. Is it so bad to celebrate your engagement under the soft glow of candlelight in a secluded corner of a quaint restaurant? I read in the paper there are a few restaurants staying open for the festive holiday."

Sophia smiled. Her mother's words always brought encouragement to Sophia's doubting heart.

"You are right, Mammá."

For a little while, no one said anything, each one seeming lost in thought. Spurts of scented pine popped from the burning logs.

Mrs. Baird broke the silence. "My dear, how does it feel to be engaged to the most handsome, eligible bachelor in town?"

Sophia didn't want the events involving her dress to cast a shadow over her engagement day. She turned to Mrs. Baird. "It feels wonderful," she said, suddenly ashamed that she had allowed recent events to darken the most wonderful day of her life.

"He's very lucky to get you, Sophia. You will make a wonderful wife."

"Thank you, Mammá."

They talked happily about Clayton and what the future might hold for the young couple. Sophia became so engrossed in their conversation, she almost forgot about the ball until a light knock sounded at the front door, and she heard Abigail burst through the door, almost out of breath.

Abby stood in the entrance of the sitting room with a box in her hands. Her cheeks flamed red against her wide smile. "This is for you, Sophia. Merry Christmas!"

twenty-two

Sophia looked from Abigail to the box. "Abby, this is for me?" The large package baffled her. Sophia couldn't imagine what was inside.

Abigail nodded heartily. She quickly pushed through the sitting room door and coaxed Sophia over to a chair to open it while Mammá and Mrs. Baird looked on.

"Go ahead, open it."

Surprised, Sophia looked at her mother, who returned the expression. Gently, Sophia lifted the lid of the box and let out a sharp cry. But for the crackling fireplace, the room grew silent. Slowly, Sophia lifted the contents from the box. A beautiful, navy blue gown emerged and tumbled to the floor in a trail of delicate ruffles and lace.

"Oh, my," Mrs. Baird and Mammá whispered.

Before anyone could say anything, Abigail began, "I bought this for you when I went with my parents to New York. Although I knew you were making another dress, I could not pass this one up. Mother and I decided you had to wear this dress. It was perfect for you. I had planned to give it to you for the ball, but you already had your heart set on the other one, and I didn't want to spoil it for you. I had no idea what I was going to do with the dress until you explained your problem this afternoon. That's why I ran out of the house. Do you like it?"

Sophia stared at her incredulously. "Like it?" She threw her arms around Abigail. "Abby, it's perfect! Far better than any dress I could dream up!"

The two friends shared an enormous hug. When they pulled away, Sophia wiped the tears from her cheeks and looked at

Abigail, who was doing the same. They both laughed.

Mammá went over to Sophia and whispered, "Did I not tell you the Lord would help us?"

"Oh, Mammá." Sophia hugged her mother, then reached out to Mrs. Baird, who was looking on.

Mrs. Baird gave Sophia a squeeze, then said, "Are you going stand here blubbering all day, or are you going to try it on?"

Everyone laughed. Sophia and Abigail placed the dress back in the box and ran upstairs with it.

ଚ

Sophia felt her heart would burst as her mother placed the gold locket around her neck, adding a delicate beauty to the lacy neckline of her evening gown. Mammá kissed her on the cheek and gave her an approving nod.

Sophia cast one last glance at her reflection, then willed her stomach to settle down. Her mother followed her to the top of the stairs. Mrs. Baird was talking with Clayton below.

Sophia stood at the top of the stairs and tried to stop trembling. Clayton's gaze lifted, and their eyes locked as she descended the steps. Her dress swished softly behind her, making her feel like a princess.

Clayton approached the bottom of the stairway to meet her. For Sophia, the look in his eyes made everything leading up to this moment worthwhile. He reached for her hand and pulled her to his side. "You look positively breathtaking."

"Thank you." Sophia smiled, wondering if she had ever felt so elegantly dressed.

Mammá straightened the back of Sophia's gown. "You two enjoy your evening," she said, giving them each a light embrace. Mrs. Baird walked over and offered the same.

As they exited the house, Sophia was sure a magic carriage awaited them.

ଚ

The large room was alive with colorful silks, sparkling jewels, and Christmas greens. A chill of anticipation shivered down Sophia's spine as she took in the view. Garlands of holly and ivy were draped in swags around long tables holding silver trays of dainty sandwiches, pastries, and bowls of bright red punch. Couples danced across the floor, sending the scent of sweet perfumes to swirl around the room.

Abigail's arm rested lightly upon Jonathan's as she motioned for Sophia and Clayton when they entered the ballroom.

Before Abigail and Jonathan reached them, Sophia looked up in time to lock eyes with Mary Nottinger. Mary gracefully strolled their way.

"Hello, Clayton. So good to see you." She grabbed his arm possessively and threw a sneer at Sophia. "Clayton, you will dance with me on this song, won't you? I've been positively dying for you to get here." She batted her eyelashes for emphasis.

Sophia felt her stomach tying in knots again.

"I'm sorry, Mary. All my dances belong to my fiancée."

"What?" Mary's face reflected absolute horror.

"Yes," Clayton said earnestly. He reached over to grab Sophia's hand. "Allow me to introduce you to my future bride, Sophia Martone."

Sophia stepped up beside him, feeling her cheeks must surely match the color of the punch.

"Well, I never!" Mary turned and stomped off in a huff.

"Does that mean she doesn't approve?" Sophia asked behind a gloved hand.

"It does indeed, my love." He laughed.

"Oh, there's my cousin," Abigail said, turning toward a handsome young man who walked their way. "Patrick, so glad you could make it." She pulled him into a hug. She turned to her friends. "Sophia, Clayton, Jonathan, this is my dear cousin, Patrick O'Connor."

After the introductions, Abigail informed them Patrick was single, twenty-five years old, and had just moved to Chicago after accepting a lucrative position with the railroad.

Before they had a chance to discuss anything further, Mary Nottinger placed herself within the group. "Patrick, I couldn't help but overhear Abigail. I wanted to be among the first to welcome you to Chicago." She offered her brightest smile before turning to Abigail. "You and Jonathan go on with your dancing. I will be most happy to introduce Mr. O'Connor to the others."

Abigail gaped as Mary pulled a puzzled Patrick into the crowd. Abigail turned to her friends. They all started laughing.

Clayton looked at Sophia. "Shall we dance?" Sophia glanced at Abigail, who was already gliding across the floor with Jonathan. She lifted her arms and followed Clayton's graceful steps, her heart feeling as light as a drifting snowflake. She knew the memories of this day would last her a lifetime.

When the song ended, a couple of Clayton's friends started conversing with him. Sophia excused herself to get some punch. While she stood in line, Mrs. Nottinger approached her.

"Sophia, so good to see you, Dear." The older woman twisted a handkerchief in her hands. Her eyes nervously scanned the room.

"Are you all right, Mrs. Nottinger?" Sophia felt sure Mrs. Nottinger would faint right on the spot.

"Could I speak to you privately?" she asked in a shaky voice.

"Of course." Sophia excused herself from the line and followed Mary's mother out of the room into a private hallway.

"I cannot live with myself for another minute." She paced back and forth, twisting the handkerchief tighter with every step. "I was wrong, and I want you to forgive me. I don't know what possessed me to do such a thing. It's just that I want what's best for my daughter, and I had such plans for her and—"

Before she could continue, Sophia stopped her. "Mrs.

Nottinger, I'm not sure I understand. What are you talking about?"

Alice Nottinger's face turned chalky white. Then, as if she pulled the words from deep within herself and pushed them out with great effort, she croaked, "I did it."

"Did what?"

"Mary told me about your gown and its beauty. She was terribly upset, crying and carrying on that Clayton was taking you and not her. I discretely plied her with questions until I found out where you kept the dress. I didn't want her to know what I was up to. This was my one last hope of getting you out of Clayton's life and Mary into it.

"I went to your shop, not really knowing what I was going to do. I walked around the back and noticed the door was ajar." She swallowed hard, the words struggling to get out. "Well, it seemed the opportunity for which I was looking, so I slipped in and took your dress."

Sophia stared at her, wide-eyed. It took her a full minute to comprehend what Mrs. Nottinger had said.

Before Sophia could respond, Mrs. Nottinger hurried on. "I panicked. I thought if I kept you from the ball—from Clayton—Mary would have a chance." She fidgeted with her fingers. "Don't you see? With you out of the picture, she did have a chance. At least, that's what I thought." Her words finally quieted to a whisper. "But now I know Clayton is in love with you."

"I see." Sophia looked down at the floor.

"Sophia, you can tell the police. Do whatever you feel is right. No one knows I did it. Not even Mary."

Sophia was surprised at that. She felt a little better, knowing Mary didn't know. Secretly, she had thought Mary might have taken it.

"I have the dress at home and will gladly return it to you."

Sophia stood for a moment, thinking. "There's no harm done, Mrs. Nottinger. Return the dress to me tomorrow, and we'll forget this incident ever happened."

Relief washed over the older woman's face. Tears sprang to her eyes. She grabbed Sophia's hands. "A mother will do almost anything for her child, but I was wrong. Thank you for forgiving me." She cupped the side of Sophia's face. "God bless you."

This time, Sophia thought the older woman really meant it.

Mr. Nottinger called to his wife, and she turned to go.

Sophia sighed with relief. With the mystery of the dress solved, she could enjoy her evening.

Clayton came into the hall. "Are you all right?"

"Yes, I'm fine now." She would tell him about the dress later, but she didn't want to talk about it just now. At this moment, all she wanted was to enjoy their evening together. Clayton grabbed her hand and swept her back onto the dance floor.

He lifted her chin to him as they moved across the polished hardwood. "It's amazing how God has worked through our relationship."

Sophia nodded.

"And to think it all started with your trunk." Love gleamed in his eyes.

"Papá always called it a trunk of surprises."

Clayton smiled. "It is indeed."

Light notes danced upon violin strings and circled around the ballroom. Clayton cupped Sophia's waist gently with one hand and guided her with the other, making her feel like a swan's feather being lifted by a puff of air. As she stared into the dark, warm eyes of the man she loved, her heart flooded with complete happiness.

Over the past several months, God's plan for her life had unfolded like a velvety, red rose stretching in the morning sun. His design for her had reached far beyond what she could have ever dreamed for herself. A smile formed on her lips.

"What's so amusing?" Clayton questioned, his eyes glinting with mischief.

"I was thinking about what you said, that it all started with the trunk. Then I thought of how God has brought us this distance together and how He seemed to have His own—"

"Trunk of surprises?" he interrupted.

She looked at him with a start. "How did you know what I was thinking?"

"Didn't you know that when people fall in love, they start thinking alike?"

"Oh, really?" She cocked an eyebrow with a mischievous look that matched his.

Clayton tipped his head back and laughed heartily as they merrily made their way around the room. Sophia joined him in the laughter. Her heart overflowed with the anticipation of tomorrows bright with the promise of love, laughter, dreams, and never-ending surprises.

A Letter To Our Readers

Dear Reader:

In order that we might better contribute to your reading enjoyment, we would appreciate your taking a few minutes to respond to the following questions. We welcome your comments and read each form and letter we receive. When completed, please return to the following:

Rebecca Germany, Fiction Editor
Heartsong Presents
PO Box 719
Uhrichsville, Ohio 44683

1. Did you enjoy reading *Trunk of Surprises* by Diann Hunt?
   ❑ Very much! I would like to see more books by this author!
   ❑ Moderately. I would have enjoyed it more if

   _____

   _____

   _____

2. Are you a member of **Heartsong Presents**?   ❑ Yes   ❑ No
   If no, where did you purchase this book? _____

   _____

3. How would you rate, on a scale from 1 (poor) to 5 (superior), the cover design? _____

4. On a scale from 1 (poor) to 10 (superior), please rate the following elements.

   ____ Heroine   ____ Plot
   ____ Hero   ____ Inspirational theme
   ____ Setting   ____ Secondary characters

6. How has this book inspired your life?_____

_____

_____

7. What settings would you like to see covered in future
   Heartsong Presents books? _____

_____

_____

8. What are some inspirational themes you would like to see
   treated in future books? _____

_____

_____

9. Would you be interested in reading other **Heartsong
   Presents** titles? ❑ Yes ❑ No

10. Please check your age range:
    ❑ Under 18   ❑ 18-24
    ❑ 25-34   ❑ 35-45
    ❑ 46-55   ❑ Over 55

Name_____

Occupation _____

Address _____

City_____ State_____ Zip_____

E-mail_____

Hearts♥ng

Any 12
Heartsong
Presents titles
for only
$30.00*

HISTORICAL ROMANCE IS CHEAPER BY THE DOZEN!

Buy any assortment of twelve *Heartsong Presents* titles and save 25% off of the already discounted price of $3.25 each!

*plus $2.00 shipping and handling per order and sales tax where applicable.

HEARTSONG PRESENTS TITLES AVAILABLE NOW:

(If ordering from this page, please remember to include it with the order form.)

······· **Presents** ·······

Great Inspirational Romance at a Great Price!

Heartsong Presents books are inspirational romances in contemporary and historical settings, designed to give you an enjoyable, spirit-lifting reading experience. You can choose wonderfully written titles from some of today's best authors like Peggy Darty, Sally Laity, Tracie Peterson, Colleen L. Reece, Debra White Smith, and many others.

$\mathcal{H}$EARTSONG ❤ PRESENTS

Love Stories Are Rated G!

That's for godly, gratifying, and of course, great! If you love a thrilling love story but don't appreciate the sordidness of some popular paperback romances, **Heartsong Presents** is for you. In fact, **Heartsong Presents** is the only inspirational romance book club featuring love stories where Christian faith is the primary ingredient in a marriage relationship.

Sign up today to receive your first set of four, never-before-published Christian romances. Send no money now; you will receive a bill with the first shipment. You may cancel at any time without obligation, and if you aren't completely satisfied with any selection, you may return the books for an immediate refund!

Imagine. . .four new romances every four weeks—two historical, two contemporary—with men and women like you who long to meet the one God has chosen as the love of their lives. . .all for the low price of $10.99 postpaid.

To join, simply complete the coupon below and mail to the address provided. **Heartsong Presents** romances are rated G for another reason: They'll arrive Godspeed!

YES! Sign me up for Hearts❤ng!

NEW MEMBERSHIPS WILL BE SHIPPED IMMEDIATELY!
Send no money now. We'll bill you only $10.99 post-paid with your first shipment of four books. Or for faster action, call toll free 1-800-847-8270.

NAME _____

ADDRESS _____

CITY _____ STATE _____ ZIP _____

MAIL TO: HEARTSONG PRESENTS, P.O. Box 721, Uhrichsville, Ohio 44683
or visit www.heartsongpresents.com